# WHERE
# PIGEONS
# GO TO DIE

# WHERE PIGEONS GO TO DIE

## R. Wright Campbell

Rawson Associates Publishers, Inc. / New York

Library of Congress Cataloging in Publication Data

Campbell, R. Wright.
  Where pigeons go to die.

  I.  Title.
PZ4.C1888Wh   [PS3553.A4867]      813'.5'4      77-94146
ISBN 0-89256-058-4

Published simultaneously in Canada by
McClelland and Stewart, Ltd.
Manufactured in the United States of America
by The Book Press, Inc., Brattleboro, Vermont
Designed by *e. o'connor*
Second Printing August 1978

*To Lynn for her independent spirit and constant searching; for autumn memories.*

# WHERE PIGEONS GO TO DIE

# Prologue

People and pigeons are curiously much alike. That is to say the lovely birds have those qualities of fidelity, affection, and love, courage, determination, and pride which are qualities humans may boast of when they are at their best. If they display jealousy and pettishness, quarrelsome moments and gluttony they should be forgiven, for their sins are small. Indeed, we humans should be forgiven as well.

In some things they shame us, by and large. Once mated, they are wed for life unless forcibly separated. When set to the task, such as a long race, they will persevere and endure through measures of hell that only the best of men will willingly undertake.

It might be argued that they are simply, dumbly, following the programing of instinct; that they can do nothing differently. Perhaps that can be said of us as well.

I've come back to the little saltbox house on the banks of one of the many streams that once fed the Genesee, summoned again by attorneys with new offers of purchase in their pockets. This old neighborhood, once semirural, has been swallowed up by the city of Rochester, New York, and is no longer the locus of my childhood: is, instead, a modern banality of apartment dwellings and condominiums; even the words are insults to my memories.

I've returned with no small sense of guilt. *I* am the one who's left Grandpere's house to strangers these last twenty years. I'm the one who's left it vacant and abandoned to weed and rot these last five. I'm the agent of its sorry neglect and destruction.

The Victorian house that once belonged to old Mrs. Chalmers, who was said to be quite dotty because of a tragic love affair and who sported a fascinating glass eye, blue and staring, acquired after a curious accident involving a hummingbird, has long since been torn down. The house was torn down soon after her death. Because she had no heirs her property was left to the state. The city of Rochester, by petition, had the dwelling declared an attractive nuisance and razed it to the ground. My father hadn't been one of those who'd signed the necessary documents. My father respected old things. I have resisted similar petitions to flatten the saltbox for no sensible reason that I can declare. Except I, too, respect the past and those who dwelt in it.

I've long since sold off the larger house left to me by my mother and father, yet, somehow have not wanted to give up this old wreck in which I'd never actually lived but which seems to be my home more than any other that's ever sheltered me. I think I was a boy here and nowhere else, became grown-up here and nowhere else.

It sits now, deprived of its once-fashionable apron of porch that surrounded it on all four sides. A rickety makeshift of stairs and a single newel post remain where once broad steps led up to the front door. Men passing by of an evening would stop to chat with my grandfather, placing one foot on a step above the other, resting their bent arms on their legs, meaning to tarry only a little while. They often talked on till their wives or children came looking for them to bring them in to supper.

Oddly, the knee-high picket fence and gate that surrounds the front yard has been kept painted and in good repair. I wonder if the owners of the concrete-block and brick buildings on either side do at least that much to shame me—the absentee owner of the eyesore —into selling out as any decent man would do —according to their lights. I don't deny them their annoyance, even anger with me.

There seems to be no path from gate to door at first and then I notice, traced with a ghostly brush charged with shadow, the walkway worn through the grass over the years. Our marks are not so easily erased. My grandfather taught me that. I have no desire to go into the house right off, I go around the back instead.

The yard is filled with rubbish, the garage atilt and threatening to fall flat in the next high wind. I feel a stone in my chest. The land is wild and overgrown, brown and yellow in the season; the willows and cottonwoods have been cut down and uprooted; the stream is gone, its bed fashioned into a culvert lined with concrete.

I start to run down the slope, kicking the pollen of the weeds into the air, afraid, now that I'm half a century old, to recall the tenth year of my life. The loft house still stands and I run to it.

In its day the pigeon loft of Henri Baudoum was a marvel, a miniature mansion of many spindled windows, porches, gables, and carved eaves. Its roofs were tiled in dusty red shingles and the trap doors were painted a shade of blue my grandfather, whom I called Da, told me was a favorite color for such decoration back in his native Belgium. It had been, in many ways, a better house than the one in which the human owners lived.

Now it is weathered to a sad grayness, paint all peeled away, shingles missing in great patches, exposing the understructure of the roof like ribs showing through the fatal wounds in the flanks of some great beast. The dowels have been ripped from nearly every window, the traps torn away, the nest boxes inside filled with garbage. Graffiti, senseless and obscene, has been carved and painted on the walls. All is ruin.

"Oh, Da," I hear myself say, and a small wind scented with the cress and wild berries that once grew by the running stream, no longer there, rises up and chokes my heart with memory, hurting me, bringing tears to my eyes.

I am ten years old again, the cardinal year of my life, and it is a day that marks the end of my childhood.

# One

I was up in the dark of four o'clock. It was late in May, but the morning was chilly all the same. I went into the bathroom and wiped a rag across my eyes, ran wet fingers through my hair and swished some water through my teeth. When I tiptoed past my mother's and father's bedroom I didn't notice that the door was somewhat ajar until my mother called out softly to me. I'd been as quiet as I knew how, yet she'd heard me. I never could understand how she, and father to a lesser degree, could awaken from the deepest sleep when I got up in the night to use the toilet or get a glass of water. Instinct of some kind, I supposed, much like the kind of stirring I felt if there was a weasel or fox skulking about the pigeon loft or one of the birds was about to come down with some sickness that hadn't yet shown itself.

I went down the dark stairs to the kitchen where I turned on the light. She followed me, all tousled with the funny, soft, bruised look around her eyes and mouth which she had when she first woke up—or when she'd been crying about something. I wondered if women commonly cried silently in their sleep. Da once said—if I remember correctly—that mothers and abandoned wives wept in the night so to wash and freshen their smiles for the day. My grandfather was sometimes given to excessively poetic and extravagant expression, had once hungered to be a man of letters. A Poet.

My mother's eyes glittered with the remains of such weightless tears as she smiled sleepily at me and brushed my hair away from my eyes.

"You should let me comb it," she said.

"It's Saturday," I reminded her and she nodded.

That was the agreement between us. I allowed her to polish my appearance every morning but Saturday and that was my own to be as rough and uncaring as I pleased.

"Big day," she whispered softly.

She shivered and made a noise with her lips.

"I never will understand why grown men will get up long before the crack of dawn—in the very middle of the night in fact—just to fool around with a bunch of birds," she said and smiled at me.

I knew she was making me proud of myself for being only ten but included in the activities of my grandfather and his friends, calling me a grown man among grown men; boasting of me for having the grit to follow my pastime with devotion despite the hardships of it. Of course there were other children and some women who raced pigeons, but even so she was proud of me.

She made me a bowl of hot farina, dressed with a pat of butter and a sprinkling of salt. She pointed to the chair beside the kitchen table and, when I didn't sit in it, put her hand on my shoulder and sat me down before I could protest that I had no time.

"Will you feed the birds this morning?" she asked.

"Yes," I said.

"Then I'll feed you," she smiled.

She poured a glass of milk for me and stood watching me as I drank it. She wore the robe I'd helped my father pick out for her birthday two years before, faded now with many washings, the little tufts depleted and some nearly worn away. It was rose-colored; reflected on her face, the slope of her cheeks, beneath her chin making her look flushed and too young to have a child. I do believe that consideration came to me that morning when I was ten.

"Keep warm," she said to me at the door, pulled the collar of my jacket up around my ears and kissed me on the corner of my mouth. "It's May but chilly all the same."

I went off to Da's house, the little saltbox about half a mile down the road. An owl spoke in the dark. Its screech identified it to me as a common barn owl, a bird that lived comfortably in the habitations of men. It lived on woodland rodents, rats, and mice. It was no danger to pigeons and other birds. I called back, but the owl was seeking no further conversation and remained silent.

I could then—as I can now rarely do— identify the calls of nearly all the avifauna for miles around. I'd learned it bit by bit, without struggle, without reluctance, as naturally as I'd learned my name, Hugh Baudoum. I have never learned anything else quite so painlessly. Perhaps because I've never since relished learning for the pure joy of it. I remember Da saying, "Knowledge made tasty creates an appetite for more. Force feeding, on the other hand, turns the stomach."

I saw a patch of violets gleaming beside the road and picked a small bunch of them. I gave them to my grandfather without embarrassment. There was no restriction on the giving of beauty as far as he was concerned, no set of actions suitable for girls and another suitable for boys.

He thanked me, put them in a glass of water and placed it on the kitchen windowsill above the sink where another water glass held his teeth.

I never liked to see him without them, though I never told him so. His mouth looked all pursed and shrunken, his cheeks without shape or fire, so old that it frightened me. He was sometimes thoughtless about his teeth in the house, but I never saw him elsewhere without them.

"Are we ready for the big day?" he lisped.

"As ready as we'll ever be," I said in ritual answer.

He popped in his teeth, nodded, grinned and said, "Then there's not a thing that can shame us."

We had a cup of herb tea, which I never drank at home, and went down to the lofts. There was light in the eastern sky. We went through the back of the house among the nest boxes and took up Jenny, Moonbeam, and Dickens, and placed them in a wicker basket partitioned into three parts.

The loft doors in front were opened then, the birds let free for the morning fly. Together, Da and I cleaned out the pans and refreshed them with new water as the pigeons flung themselves about the sky. We set out the grain mix in the hopper and I called the pigeons back to feed by snapping a metal cricket. In fifteen minutes or so they began, one by one, to leave the feed and go to drink. When everyone had enough, but not too much, we cleared out the hoppers. That day we left the doors open, allowing the birds the freedom of the air, the roof, the several porches, and went off in Da's pickup truck with the birds that were to race.

The fanciers were gathering in the clubhouse of the Rochester American Racing Pigeon Union. It was half past six and already the room was growing thick with the heat of so many bodies. The smell of tobacco, coffee, and the peculiarly dusty, acrid odor of bird droppings laced the air. The men and a few women—who tended to be the sturdy, hardy sort—jostled each other in friendly companionship, talking pigeons and bragging on one bird or another. There were some children my own age among us. Most were bigger than I, for I was undersized for a ten-year-old. Harry Pinnat waved to me, showing the gap in his smile where he'd lost a tooth in a fight with his best friend Roger Drinier over some matter concerning pigeon bloodlines.

We young ones were a serious lot I suppose. I've noticed since that youngsters brought up around creatures tend to be a trifle more mature and dependable than others. Anyway we'd much rather listen to the talk of our elders, and even join in the conversation when asked, than gabble among ourselves or play the fool at childish games. The talk was always plainspoken but somehow quite exotic.

"She was my pet. Wry-tailed, roach-backed, and foul-marked. I should have culled her from the flock when I brought the young birds to conclusion that first September—she wasn't steady and liked to bum around the countryside instead of making straight for the loft—but, somehow, I had hopes for her. She proved herself the very next year in two- and three-hundred-mile races."

I understood that the fancier was speaking of a bird with a tail held off to one side, round-shouldered, with off-colored feathers, who'd shown very bad habits in the first year of training and had nearly been chopped from the flock. Now she was a winner and a favorite. The fancier felt affectionate toward her, as many did toward a wayward or gadling who'd given up their wastrel ways and made something of themselves. It proved out the instinctive wisdom and bird-sense enjoyed by the fancier.

Bad habits, like wandering about instead of flying straight home, weren't to be allowed. Such birds were good for neither racing nor breeding and were killed—some hearts would say ruthlessly—in order to protect the quality of the bloodline. No breeder enjoyed the task, but they felt it necessary. They wouldn't otherwise take the life of a bird. There *were* stories, however, that aroused the anger of good pigeon fanciers.

Like the one my grandfather told that was said to have happened in 1930.

There was no need to establish any background to the tale as far as most of those who listened were concerned, but my grandfather sketched it all the same, just in case someone who didn't know a thing about pigeon racing might fail to get the message.

"You know," he'd begin in his light Walloon accent, "that the speed of each bird is measured from the time of its release to the

14

time its leg band is removed and placed in the automatic clock given to each trainer. That number is divided into the true, surveyed airline distance from start to loft and the speed in yards per minute computed.''

''Do we need instruction?'' old Mr. Fouquet, himself a man of Flanders, murmured under his breath. He was Da's best friend in all the world—next to me.

''In a racing club in Pennsylvania—''

''What club?'' Fouquet demanded.

My grandfather placed a finger beneath his eye and closed the lid of it, a lock upon a secret.

''—there was a man named Deegan, Deighton, Dugan, or such like,'' Da said without pause, ''who owned a bird named Skeeter, Tweeter, Jeeter, or such like.''

''You have a remarkable memory, Baudoum.''

''I am a man of discretion,'' Da said. ''This bird was entered into a five-hundred-mile race. There was a first prize of one hundred dollars. Skeeter—''

''Jeeter, Tweeter, or such like.''

''—came to Deegan's—''

''—Dugan's or Deighton's—''

''—loft in plenty of time to win. But it would not trap.''

Collective sighing often greeted this information. Who among us hadn't suffered the suspense of waiting for a bird to enter the little one-way door into the loft where it could be taken in hand, the countermark on the band removed and placed in the clock to mark the finish of its race? Who hadn't lost one or two races because of a stubborn, nervous, or badly trained bird?

"The bird wouldn't enter the loft. It dawdled about on the roof, sashayed around the porch, but nimbly eluded every attempt its owner made to take it in hand."

The listeners nodded. They'd all been irked by birds that played coy and would not allow themselves to be taken up and held.

"Now the year was 1930, the depression at its height, the fancier without work or money to pay his bills, and the damn bird was teasing him with a hundred dollars just out of arm's reach. If he made a grab the bird might fly, and it seemed to him that every second lost was losing him the race and the prize."

Da would light his pipe then, letting the suspense grow in little bubbles of pent breath.

"What finally happened?" Fouquet would finally insist, though he'd heard the story many times.

"The fancier went to his house where he kept a shotgun, came back, shot the bird, removed the countermark, placed it in the clock and collected the prize money."

"Why'd you keep quiet about the crime?" Fouquet would demand.

"Who am I to judge the harshness of a man's need?" Da would say and look at me. "He had his own road to walk. It wasn't for me to say how wrongly he'd placed his feet."

In this way of parable and metaphor I gathered much instruction from my grandfather in a simple and lasting way. He liked to tell stories and I liked to listen. We went together well.

The talk of pigeons filled the clubhouse. Music to me.

"I start training youngsters as soon as they've thrown their second flight. The first toss is at two miles, then four, eight, twelve, sixteen, twenty-four. Then twice at forty and twice at sixty," one fancier said.

"My birds, three years and over, get the same training as my yearlings except before long races. Then I toss them later in the day about fifteen miles out from the loft so they'll be homing in about eight twenty, just as it starts growing dark," another offered.

I'd heard all of this many times before, yet I listened quietly and with interest. Some things aren't learned really well until they've been repeated so often that they seep into the bones. I knew that was so. My grandfather had told me.

"I mate my birds on February tenth to the day, at noon to the hour. I allow them to raise one pair of youngsters for three weeks."

Da moved away from the gossip and was stopped almost at once by another pocket of men. I stayed by his side.

"What do you say, Baudoum?" John Purley, who had a wooden leg, asked.

"About what? You know my grandson, do you, John?"

The big man looked down at me and reached forth his hand. It was big and gentle. We shook man to man. I felt good for it.

"I do," John said. "Are you entered, Hugh?"

"I'm flying Dickens," I said.

John nodded and gave back his attention to my grandfather.

"What do you say about using the Widower Method over short distances?"

"Don't hold with it," Da said. "There's something cruel and foolish about getting a bird all het up and then whisking him away from his lady. How'd you like it, John, if you were plucked away from Harriet on a cold night out of a warm bed?"

Everyone laughed softly.

It's a curious fact about children brought up around animals, whether farm or sporting stock, that they are soon sophisticated in matters of creature sexuality long before they can easily apply the information to human affairs. Such jokes often pass over their heads with a rather bewildering flutter of laughter. It's then they know that, for all the fact of adult treatment in most matters, they are children still. At least those who hold great store by child innocence would hope so. I recall wondering about the cause of the laughter. There was nothing funny about being taken from a warm bed.

I was well aware of the details of the

18

method referred to as the "Widower" which was used to key up male birds just before a race. The customary procedure was to remove the cock from his mate three or four days before the flight and confine him out of sight of his nest box. Just before he was to be taken off for shipment to the starting site, he was allowed a brief visit with his wife, to dance and murmur before her in seductive invitation only to be whisked away before consummation and deposited in the shipping basket. His anxiety to return to his hen often produced flashing performances on the flight home.

"Too many of those segregated birds fall into unnatural habits," Da said, "and such practices will spread through an entire loft."

"What about jealousy?" John asked.

Da looked at me.

"Hugh tried it with one of his birds not long ago. What did you think, son?"

I considered the question as carefully as some old cracker-barrel philosopher ten times my age.

The jealousy plan was similar in effect but somewhat different in execution. While the cock was confined within sight of his nest, an aggressive male was put in with his mate. The dispossessed bird was made unhappy, fearful, and enraged. Such driving emotions were intended to, and did, produce flights of great speed as the bird exerted itself to return to the loft quickly enough to save his home and marriage.

"Don't hold with it, neither," I finally said

in miniature expression of my grandfather's manner. "It makes for nervous birds who go easily off their feed."

Da nodded and smiled, pleased with my response.

"Best things for cocks, short races or long, is to fly them back to youngsters in the nest three weeks or eggs a few days old," he said.

"Hens do better flying to eggs ten days old," I offered.

"Some return best to youngsters five or ten days old," Da added. He glanced at me and smiled, squinting up his eyes as though to say, "When these fellas want to know about pigeons, they come to the Baudoums."

I've been sitting in the dry grass, resting my back against the loft, facing the house. I'm looking toward the hills beyond it. At least I imagine they are still there. My view of those hills, which I recall with such affection, is obscured by another apartment building, monolithic and prisonlike.

I examine the name Baudoum, my own name, and my father's, but more my grandfather's than any other's. That's to say that my father, like myself, was an American who happened to bear a foreign, exotic, and euphonious last name. Da, however, was a Belgian and, though English came to be his language far more than the French of his youth, the accents of the town of Havelange in the plateau country of Condroz had been as rich as cream on his tongue. His was a curious speech; accented but fashioned in a Yankee way, product of his long years as a traveling man selling foundry type to newspapers and printing shops in New England and along the eastern seaboard.

I, in common with most of us who find ourselves growing old, especially those of us who find ourselves alone, without progeny or heirs, have suddenly become most interested in my heritage. I've no intention of trying to trace my line back to some bastard beggar of the fourteenth century or even to some ancient noble; it's enough that I should know something more of my grandfather and *his* grandfather. No more than that.

I know that my *great*-grandfather was born in Havelange in the year 1840. He was baptized Etienne. At the age of ten he was apprenticed to a shoemaker of the town and married the master's daughter when he was twenty and she sixteen. Her name was Sophie. She was delivered of seven children; Henri, the second of them, born in 1862, the only one to break with his background and reach out for opportunity, was my grandfather.

He sometimes spoke to me of his life in Belgium in a way that wasn't meant to instruct or even entertain, detached and somehow wondering as though he vaguely perceived that he'd cut himself adrift from his past and suffered for it. I feel now, looking back on those times and analyzing his feelings as he expressed them, and mine as I listened but understood imperfectly, that he wanted me to value the time we spent together because it would serve me well when I was grown in special ways that words could not describe. When he spoke of his own grandfathers it was with a sense of loss; he hadn't been at home when either of them had died.

My mother's father and mother had moved to the Midwest before I was born. I'd seen them from time to time, but they were remote to me. I could understand what Da felt. My grandmother, Jenny, Da's wife, was already dead before I was old enough to know, and that loss was distanced as well. I understood that talking of his forebears didn't really make them live again for him because he'd not been there to "weave cloth with them."

But if Da had no people to remember fully from his past, I am less fortunate because I have none at all to journey with into the future. The thought brings a terrible melancholy to my heart. I seek refuge in that racing day.

# *Two*

I leaned against my grandfather's leg. I was growing a bit sleepy from the closeness of the clubhouse and the inactivity after so much bustle getting there.

Da placed his hand on my shoulder, sensing my weariness. He often knew my moods before I was fully aware of them. The murmurous sound of so many voices was enough to put nearly anyone to sleep.

"How many are you flying, Baudoum?" someone asked.

"Three. Jenny, Moonbeam, and Hugh's own, Dickens."

"Why are you flying so few?"

"We've had quantity," Da smiled. "Now we want quality above all else."

"I'm tossing twelve birds," a fancier said.

"That's all well and good," Da grinned, "but will they fly?"

There was general laughter at his sally. Pleasurable and respectful. I was pleased to know that breeders and trainers with more money and bigger lofts, twenty times the birds and ten times the means, still looked to my grandfather in matters concerning the science and sport of pigeon racing.

"Baudoum!" The name was called from the long table where the club secretary sat. Da jostled me and sent me off to watch the examination of our birds for disease.

"That's a good fellow you've got there," I heard someone remark before I was out of earshot.

"I didn't have all that much time when my own boy was that age. It's one of the few pleasures of growing old to have a second chance with a boy like that," I heard Da say.

I checked in at the secretary's desk, paid the fees, received the countermark slips, and signed in on the entry sheet.

"Is Dickens fit?" the secretary teased.

I considered that for a time. "If Dickens doesn't win, he'll have done his best," I finally said. I went back to stand in companionable silence with my grandfather, knowing I'd answered as he would have done.

After a bit our name was called again. We went to retrieve our birds in the small wicker baskets and took them to another long table.

The clerk checked each bird off the entry sheet, assigned it a countermark number read off a rubber leg band, and placed the band on the bird. The numbers were noted on the slips of paper I'd been given.

A time clock, set and sealed, was handed

over to me along with three capsules. As each bird arrived back at the loft, the countermark and the slip of paper were to be placed in a metal capsule and cranked into the clock which marked the time on it. Three signatures of club committeemen crossed the seal to guard against any tampering.

I watched everything with a sense of greater vividness than I'd ever felt before; wide awake now. It was no ordinary race we were to have but a six-hundred-mile Concourse. Something very special.

The birds were placed in shipping baskets and chalk marks numbering them put on the top of the wicker lids. Moonbeam fussed a little at the handling by strangers. Jenny was placid as always. At the last moment Dickens appeared to look right at me. He murmured throatily. I reached out a finger and touched my bird on the head, ruffling, then smoothing the feathers a bit.

I looked at my grandfather. Did he think me foolish?

"He'll do," Da said.

"He was true in the egg," I replied. I remembered the mating of my pigeon's parents.

The cock and hen had been chosen in the hope that they'd produce long-flight racers right from the very start. They were betrothed amid the soft conversation between an old man of seventy and a boy nearly six.

Da's hands, stained and carved with time to the color and texture of oak tree bark, carefully and slowly spread Lady Valiant's wing. His fingers were as tender and gentle as a girl's. They found little resistance in the wing.

"Do you see, Hugh? She gives way without a fuss. That means we should pair her with a cock that will resist the opening of its wing."

"Starcross don't open so easy," I offered.

"Indeed," Da said, "but he's long and rangy. Our Lady Valiant's short and squatty. It's not good to mate bodies so much different."

"How about Angel?"

"Better," Da smiled. "In fact he might be well nigh perfect. He likes the long flight. Let's look him over."

We found the next suitor and gave him a look.

"His eyes are dark and Lady's are dark. Do you hold to the view that dark should be bred to light?" Da asked.

I considered that for a time. Da was never hurried when asked important questions and neither would I be.

"I don't hold with it," I said finally.

"Neither do I," Da said. He examined Angel and pointed out to me that the bird's nose wattles were small and the eye ceres light, a good match to those of the hen.

His old man's big fingers explored Angel's chest, confirming what he already knew. He was making a show of weighing matters for the value of instruction in it for me. I knew him pretty well, you see.

"Breastbone seems straight enough to me. What do you say?"

My small fingers probed in the path ruffled through the feathers by my grandfather's touch. I raised my eyes to the sky for the benefit of the concentration in it.

"He's not crooked-breasted," I agreed.

"He's not," Da said. "I think he's a proper mate, don't you?"

"Indeed," I said.

I watched fascinated by the courtship that followed when Angel was put into the nest box with Lady Valiant.

The cock addressed his fine intentions to the hen, confident in his manner, prepared to be persistent in the event the lady proved to be timid before his ardor. He approached her. She stood very still, looking him over with an eye that might well be described as wary. He bowed to her courteously. It was a stately introduction, quite old-fashioned in human terms, dignified and strangely intense.

Spreading the feathers of his tail and wing, he danced little pirouettes, charming her with his delicacy and good manners. Growing bolder, he tried to press his body against her. She gave way slowly, but with some reluctance. Her demurrer was not meant to be a rebuff or refusal of new advances. As he danced he wooed her with sweet murmurings and mutterings.

All at once Lady Valiant returned his crowding caresses. Angel stood erect and became still. Lady's eyes sparkled, her neck swelled and began to pulsate almost imperceptibly, then with greater vigor. She spread the feathers of her tail and thrust out the primary feathers of flight from her wings. She clearly meant to surrender aggressively. Nodding and bobbing, she retreated invitingly a pace or two, then suddenly renewed her advances with new fervor matching Angel's ardor with her own. She attempted to place her beak into his. They kissed. She closed her eyes a bit in the fullness of the moment.

Angel's head and neck pumped and shook. Lady seemed to feed upon some sweetness within his beak. They disengaged for a breath. She turned and crouched, offering herself. Angel mounted her. Their ani touched fleetingly. The sperm was transferred without need of penetration. The marriage was consummated.

They would remain mated for life unless forcibly separated.

Angel and Lady Valiant left the nest box and sought the reaches of the sky in which to soar and dart, tumble and cut figures in rapturous nuptial flight.

Two days later Lady Valiant laid the first egg of a clutch of two at six o'clock in the late afternoon. The second—my special bird—arrived at two in the afternoon of the following day.

I stared at the egg that was to hatch into

my bird; my own special bird. It was true that all the pigeons belonged to Da and me, share and share alike, but children are sensitive in the knowledge that such partnerships are really too much the gift of the older to the younger. They think more of that thing or creature which is made a special gift: a designated responsibility.

I looked at *my* egg. It was pearly white, smooth as buffed ivory. I was certain that it was a good deal bigger than the other in the clutch. Not *too* much larger. Just enough to hint at its superiority. I think, had I been asked and if I hadn't been too much afraid of being laughed at, I would have admitted to the fact that I was quite sure that my egg glowed a bit, that it was touched with magic.

My grandfather and I would often sit, as I am sitting now a generation later, backs against the loft house, listening to the idle murmurings of the birds, dozing in the sun from time to time. He imparted little bits of history to me, using my interest in pigeons as the conduit.

He was eight and nine during the two years of the Franco-Prussian War, already a raiser of pigeons, interested in everything about them. The newspapers were filled with stories of the siege of Paris.

Before the Germans had arrived beneath its walls, eight hundred birds belonging to societies of northern France had been brought into the city. They had settled to the lofts and would home to them.

The people of Paris were isolated from the world, without means of communication, ignorant of whether or not attempts to lift the siege were afoot. On a morning in September, 1870, a balloon, the *Neptune,* left the city carrying official and civilian dispatches. But there was no way of knowing if it had managed to land safely beyond enemy lines. It was proposed, therefore, that the next balloon, the *Ville de Florence,* should take pigeons with them that could fly back with any message of success.

The sixty balloons that followed carried over two hundred pigeons out of Paris to be fitted with messages and returned when needed to impart information and lift the morale of the citizens.

During the severe winter of that year the ground was usually white with snow, obscuring the landmarks below and adding to the confusion of birds often liberated, against the advice of the pigeon fanciers, in fog and intense cold. Many were lost to weather, some to predator birds, and some to the guns of peasants who, ignorant of the use to which the pigeons were being put, shot them down for the stew pot.

I cried when the story was first told to me. I tried to stem them or, at least, conceal them as best I could, believing tears to be a sign of weakness. Who cried over the frustration of courage that had happened seven of my lifetimes past? Da had placed his hand on my hand

and reached out his clean handkerchief to me.

"It's all right, Hugh," he'd say. "A fine tribute to brave hearts."

In such ways Da made the birds quite human to me. I believed, ceased to credit it but, sitting here in this moment, believe again that the pigeons fly in answer to more than instinct. They race for honor every bit as real as that which governs men.

I feel lifted by the thought, refreshed and strengthened in spirit. I'm young again in the certainty of such magic truth, alive to a world in which all things are possible.

# *Three*

We stayed on until all the birds were banded and basketed for travel to the release site six hundred miles away in Hillsboro, Illinois. I felt that curious sense of separation that always seemed to follow the temporary loss of our racing birds, a certain letdown in the bustle of the day, an irritation with the long delay that was to follow before the message came that the birds were released and the race begun.

We walked out to my grandfather's pickup truck.

"Anything you'd like to do with the day?" Da asked.

"There's work at the lofts," I replied.

Da smiled. "The race hasn't even begun. You can't go hanging around the lofts day and night. Your mother would have my hide. Next thing you know you'll be sleeping in with the birds."

"We could get things ready for when they come home," I said.

"Dickens won't come home any faster if we stand at the door with a welcome mat."

"I mean to wait for Moonbeam and Jenny just as hard," I protested.

"Not likely," Da laughed.

"I favor them all," I insisted.

"But I think you've got a special fondness for Dickens. Isn't that so?"

I grinned. I knew my grandfather was slyly watching me out of the corner of his eye as he started the truck, waiting for my true reply.

"Indeed," I finally said, just as he would have done, after reasonable consideration, giving much and little of my feelings away.

"First thing, we'll get something to eat," Da decided.

We drove along the road that shouldered the Genesee River toward Da's house. The wind blew in through the open windows of the truck, mussing up his white hair. He half closed his eyes against it and darted them from one side of the road to the other.

"Things are changing," he said as though to himself.

"What, Da?" I said.

"Things are much changed from the time when I settled your grandmother in the house along the stream. The girls"—meaning my aunts Amelie and Agethe—"used to come out to that place right there."

I looked to see an area paved with concrete, fenced in all around with chain link fence, some sort of storage place I supposed.

"Wildflowers of a dozen sorts grew there.

It was the end of the trolley line. Seemed to be a hundred miles from home. Gone now."

"I can see."

"Yes, the flowers gone. And the girls gone too," Da said with a rare wistfulness in his voice. "Your Aunt Amy lives way out in California. Mean to go there one day. Yes, I'll do it when I can find the time. Aggie's living down in Louisiana. Should visit with her, too. I'll do it—one day."

He was quiet for a while, then the house came in sight. All of a sudden he said, "A body never gets tired of coming home, does he?"

I could feel his love of the little house, the backyard, the rushing stream, the pigeon lofts, the stand of trees, and the two small gardens that he grew, one for herbs and one for table vegetables. It was something I could almost touch.

We reached the house. Da drove the pickup along the double track of concrete that led to the garage. We got out, stood a moment, the sun warm on our faces. The river mist was all burned away since the morning when I'd walked to the house made mysterious by the foggy dark just barely tinged with dawn. Everything was quite ordinary now. I tried to feel the magic of homecoming which Da seemed to feel, but it had been too short a journey for a boy to get much homesick. Is it because a child always expects that home will be there? Does an old man fear it may not be? Of course I loved the house. It was comfortable. Familiar.

The birds had trapped themselves of their own accord. Da didn't believe in letting the birds have the complete freedom of the skies. He'd learned they actually took less exercise, hung about the porches and roofs of the lofts, gossiping instead of taking flight. They were given their freedom with the rising of sun, when it was high, and when it set. Then the river breezes stirred, ruffling the down on the birds' breasts and rousing them to joy.

We walked down to the pens. The river lay some distance away, a silver path at the end of the long slope of the valley. A stand of willows and cottonwoods had been planted as a break against any chilling winds of too much power. Their whispering created an odd windowed silence when I stood as I did facing the smoothly running water of the stream that fed the Genesee.

My grandfather freed the gates. The birds rushed out, gathered, and then took wing all in a rush. They columned into the air nearly wing to wing. A solid shape of feathers, a single hush of sound. They whipped about—leaves caught in the pools and eddies of the sky—wind-tossed.

I craned my neck to look at them, flashing white, gray opal, and grizzle blue against the vault of day. My heart lifted up. Would I ever tire of the sight? The thought, come all unbidden, somehow saddened me for a moment. I took several steps closer to my grandfather who was looking up with distance-seeking eyes such as sailors and plainsmen are said to have. They were so clearly blue as to seem to reflect the very sky itself.

With a rush of love that shook me I was sharply aware that my grandfather was feeling exactly what I felt myself. Surely I would never tire of the sight of birds set free. I took my grandfather's hand.

"We'll let them play as they like while we have something to eat," Da said.

We walked back to the house and let ourselves in through the kitchen door into the small mud room. Da stamped his feet from old habit, small ritual of remembered domesticity. I did the same. We went into the kitchen, sunny and old-fashioned. My mother kept the curtains starched and crisp at the windows despite Da's protestations that he could do without such feminine niceties. Her answer was a smile as she went on about her purpose, setting tulips and hyacinths in bright little pots around the place in proper season, braiding a small rug to place in front of the kitchen sink.

"You may pretend to be a crusty old bachelor," she would often tease, "but the fact of a marriage that lasted nearly thirty-five years kind of ruins the act, wouldn't you say?"

Da would humph or growl because he felt it expected of him. He'd sit glowering at the kitchen table, playing the role my mother Beth assigned him. When she was gone, the woman's smell of her still lingering in the room, he'd get

very quiet, his eyes strangely bright, and I knew
he was thinking of Grandma Jenny when first
they'd moved into the house with nothing more
than a bed, a table, and a few chairs. Did he
have her back with him again, young, strong-
limbed, hair as rich and heavy as shocked wheat,
the way he'd so often described her to me? In a
kitchen once furnished with nothing much more
than the sun pouring through the window did
he hold her prisoner in his arms again and kiss
her for dear life and good love as I sometimes
saw my father do to Mother?

I'd cough or make some other sound to
bring Da back to me at such times, jealous of a
past in which I'd had no part.

He stood at the window as the breeze swept
up from the river and the birds soared overhead. The look was in his eyes; I coughed.

He shook his head and smiled, then went to
the icebox and poked around inside, brought out
a big tomato and some lettuce, fried some bacon,
and toasted four slices of bread cut from a fresh
loaf. We built two rough sandwiches together.
Da found some schoolboy apples and set them
on the table with a bottle of milk and I brought
two tumblers from the drainboard by the sink.

We sat down to eat, two old fanciers having
a bite together. Comfortable. Companionable.
Prepared to eat in silence as old comrades
will.

Da had taken a first taste of the good, cold
milk when he raised his hand to his hair and

cried out as though something had smashed through his head.

I think now of how my grandfather stressed the virtue of loving one's home. As a boy I thought it because he'd been forced by circumstance to be a gadling and wanderer, an emigrant to a strange land, a salesman forced to travel in order to earn his living and support his family.

Since then I've come to know that wasn't at all the truth of it. First of all, his life in Havelange wasn't one of harsh deprivation. Nor had he ever said it was, but certain stories tended to present his childhood as one of greater hardship than it had been in reality. I've come to know it as a device by which elders boast of the better life they've managed for their sons and daughters.

Da's father had wanted better things for his eldest son, second oldest child. Henri Baudoum was given more schooling than was common to a member of the craftsman's class. It was often interrupted, and he was twenty before he finished his secondary schooling, but his father was ready to send him on to the University at Liège if Henri could pass the examinations.

My grandfather didn't try because his feet were restless. He wanted to see the world and used the money meant for his tuition to buy passage to America. That was in the year 1882,

nearly a hundred years from this day in which
I sit upon the ground beside an empty pigeon
loft and dwell on another day forty years past.

The tangle of time fascinates and con-
founds me. How can it be that I've thought so
little of that day for this long stretch of years?
Is that so? Wouldn't it be closer to the truth
were I to say that the day has never left me for
a moment? That day and the ones that followed.
Perhaps I haven't consciously dwelt on it, but
the ghost of it is in my bones and blood.

# *Four*

"My good Lord!" Da said. He dropped the glass, the milk spilling all over the flowered oilcloth. He struggled to stay upright on the straight-backed, armless wooden chair, staring at me as though waiting for an answer to some most important question. He lost the battle and toppled sideways, falling heavily to the floor.

A bolt of fear lanced through my heart. I felt a weakness in my belly and legs. I tried to move and couldn't, holding the glass in my two hands, unable to feel the icy chill of it. My stunned immobility lasted for a long moment, then I placed the glass very slowly and gently on the table, carefully avoiding the puddle Da's milk had made. Suddenly I was crying out for my grandfather, scrambling out of my chair and falling on my knees beside the old man. I picked up Da's big hand and cradled it with my own small hands against my chest, hopefully, as though cupping a bird that was apt to fly away. I wondered that my grandfather's hand felt heavy, yet fragile, at the same time. I peered into his face.

It was twisted all askew, one eye nearly closed, the other opened painfully wide in fearful surprise. He lay on the floor, moving one leg weakly but steadily, attempting to rise and restore his dignity, somehow aware of the grotesque and awkward picture he made lying there. He looked nothing like the tall strong man, craggy and eternal, I knew. Da tried to speak. A frightening crush of strangled sound came out, unintelligible, driving my fear to a terrible peak.

"What is it, Da?" I shouted.

My grandfather's eyes pleaded with me to understand. When he tried to speak again, the same sorry confusion spilled out. He strained his eyes toward the telephone, making a greater horror of the mask that had replaced his face.

I saw what he wanted. I went to the phone and called my father at the newspaper but was told that he was gone for the midday meal. I called Radner's Department store then and got my mother in the accounting department. She listened to what I told her of the accident that had befallen Da and, in her calm, soothing way, told me to wait until she arrived.

"Put a pillow under Grandpa's head and make him as comfortable as you can, Hugh. Throw a light blanket over him if he seems cold. Don't be afraid. I'm going to call for an ambulance and it may get there before I do."

Her calm soothed my racing heart somewhat. I went into Da's bedroom and took the neatly folded blanket and a pillow from the big bed. I glanced at a photograph of my grandma smiling sweetly from a silver frame. I'd never known her. Still I said, "He'll be all right."

When I returned to the kitchen, Da's eyes were closed, his breathing loud and labored. I placed the pillow beneath the heavy head, brushing back the thin white hair that fell across his brow, and placed the coverlet over him. I picked up his worn old hand again and held it to my chest. I thought of Dickens and the other pigeons traveling to the beginning of the race. Somehow in the moment I saw the trial my grandfather and Dickens faced as much the same. Both had a long way to home.

I could imagine Dickens on the way. The wicker baskets would have been distributed along the sides of the transport in order to insure good circulation of clean air on the long journey to Hillsboro, Illinois. The wicker baskets would be creaking gently with the movement of the express truck, rocking and swaying smoothly. Not many of the birds would be affrighted, for nearly all were seasoned flyers with a great number of training flights and competitions behind them. Those who were not would find comfort in the company of older, wiser birds. Dickens was wise and steady and calm. He'd had nearly four years of racing experience.

I held my grandfather and found comfort in thoughts about the birth of a pigeon.

Lady Valiant had brooded the first egg lightly. Angel took the nest, hovering the egg, from time to time. But when the second egg was laid, both cock and hen sat to incubate the clutch, Lady Valiant during the night until about nine o'clock in the morning, Angel relieving her until about three or four in the afternoon.

I spent every waking hour of the day after school was over, and many that were half asleep early in the morning or fairly late in the night, watching the birds at the birthing.

Da remarked to my mother that Lady's clutch had three sitters, herself, Angel, and me.

On the seventeenth day the first signs of pipping appeared, a small crack, a pushing upward in the middle of each shell. Both eggs showed the signs at very nearly the same moment, a rare and strange phenomenon which I chose to take—coupled with the approach of my own sixth birthday—as an incredibly favorable sign. Surely my bird, hurrying to be born, to come into the world on the birthdate of its master, was destined to be an exceptional pigeon in all regards.

On the very day when I was to be six I hurried around to the front of Da's house where my grandfather was dozing in the rocking chair upon the porch. I roused him with cries and tugs. Da stirred reluctantly from his comfort at first, then quickly roused himself to a pitch that matched my own enthusiasm. We went back together to the nest of marvels.

We watched together as the eggs trembled and shook. Da lifted my egg and held it to my ear so that I might hear it ticking away intermittently; a mysterious and priceless living timepiece.

"This is what's going on that we can't see," Da said. "Your chick, and the other, has turned itself and is pipping away at the large end of the egg. In a few hours it'll work its way around, pipping away and pushing with its shoulders against the sides until the end of the egg falls away and the egg is opened."

Da returned the egg to the nest.

The eggs hatched just before noon, just minutes before I'd been born six years before. I gave all my attention to the bird that was my own. The squab, nearly bald but spiny with damp, threadlike down, uncoiled its neck and stretched.

"Good Lord, Da," I breathed.

"Indeed," Da smiled. "Now what will you call him?"

I thought awhile, giving such an important matter my most careful consideration. Of late my grandfather had been reading to me before bedtime from the works of Charles Dickens. Such adventures as *Oliver Twist, David Copperfield* and *The Cricket on the Hearth,* excerpted, revised, and condensed here and there.

"Dickens," I finally said.

"It'll do fine, just fine," Da agreed.

That evening my mother and father took me to Da's house for a small party in my honor. When Da toasted my birthday, he toasted the birth of Dickens as well.

There was a cake and ice cream, apple cider and presents. Da gave me a red wagon with wooden sides that could be removed if one was of a mind. The body and the spinners on the rubber-tired wheels were bright red enamel and the trademark was a representation of wings in yellow upon the red.

"This wagon is practical as well as the means for some good fun," Da said. "When pigeons are taken in their baskets some distance from the loft on training flights, a trainer needs transport to get them there calm and rested."

"It's big enough for a boy twice his age, Pa," my father said.

"Can you pull it, Hugh?" Da asked and fixed me with his sky-blue eyes.

I considered the question.

"With you to help me, Da." I said.

As I held my stricken grandfather and found what comfort I could in such memories, a light breeze was riffling the surface of the water of Lake Winnepeg in Manitou. As the minutes passed, it blew harder, the wavelets showing black as the rising wind reached from shore to shore. The leaves of the trees along the banks rustled and whirled about on their stems until many were torn off. They sailed, small green kites, until they came to rest on the lake. They were swept along, small boats under full sail.

The racing clouds in the upper layers of the air proved that the winds aloft were moving at a greater speed than those below, a sign of storm in birth. The visibility was abnormally clear, promising rain. The sun heated the water, evaporation created convection currents, damp air from the lake rose several thousand feet. Large cumulus clouds formed. The atmosphere began to tumble upon itself. The wind was blowing southeast.

I can imagine all this now because I've come to know about such things as the genesis of storms. On that afternoon when I crouched in fear for my beloved grandfather, I had no idea of any such weather front moving in from Canada; was only to learn of it after the fact. It would have been of no consequence to me in that terrible moment in any event.

But, recalling all that happened means imagining that which I wasn't witness to, the winds of Lake Winnepeg, the travels and trials of my bird Dickens, even the thoughts that may have occupied my grandfather's mind as he lay helpless in the strictures of the paralysis.

# Five

The express trucks, carrying the racing pigeons to Illinois, stopped for the night in Springfield, Ohio. The baskets were unloaded from the trucks and placed in a long tractor shed, which had been rented for the one night, on the outskirts of town.

As the light faded from the sky, the birds' inner clocks ran down and they settled themselves to roost. The Rochester handlers serviced the baskets, freshening the water and renewing the grain.

Dickens pecked at a bit of it, fretting over the loss of his mate and chicks. He sensed, rather than remembered, other separations in the past. They were lonely passages best lived through quietly and then forgotten. He murmured to himself to soothe his heart and rested.

I found little to soothe my own heart.

I understood very little of the conversation I overheard between the family doctor and my parents. I sat in the corner of the waiting room feeling lost and unreal, wanting to cry but afraid to do so. My mother seemed as calm as ever, but I noticed that her fingers plucked at the lapels on her coat and there were little x's of concern between her eyes that suddenly made her look much older.

My father, too, seemed older, standing taller than the doctor and my mother, head bent, listening in the serious way that was familiar to me. In many ways my father was older than my grandfather, tending to worry more and smile less. Was it at the two ends of life that things were simplest; most joyous?

Doctor Sand murmured of clots and insults to the brain, of subdural and extradural hemorrhage. "Too soon to make a diagnosis. Too soon to tell," was the clearest of what the doctor said. Mysteries of words to me.

All I was certain of was the fact that my grandfather had suffered some outrage to his dignity and health called a stroke. Da was greatly changed. Threatened. He'd fallen on the floor and had lain there all twisted, imploring forgiveness with his eyes. Now he was lying in a strange bed and that bothered me most of all. I was certain that Da hated that. My grandfather had always made much of the pleasure of sleeping in one's own bed. He'd spent some years racketing about the country, finding cold comfort—usually—in unfamiliar nests. He said, "If anything marked a civilized man who'd earned his content it was the right and privilege to put his head down in the bed he d grown fond of or, at least, used to." A bed was a most important attribute of a home that gave everyone a center to their lives.

This is true of most creatures.

I watched Dickens growing aware of his nest. He was watched as, perhaps, no bird in history had ever been watched.

I marveled quietly at the miracle of pigeon "milk," that extraordinary substance created in the crops of both male and female for the feeding of the young. Cream-colored particles of it, much like curd, could be seen occasionally sticking to the sides of the mouths of parents and nestlings.

Dickens's tiny crop was so stuffed with the food, when first he began to feed, that it formed a ball very nearly as large as the rest of his body.

From a tiny, weak creature with wet downy feathers, eyes closed, beak wide and blindly searching, Dickens grew, in four days, into a ball of fluff quite able to sit in the nest with his head held upright. From that time on, more and more hard small-grain—millet, kafir, and wheat —fed to the parents, found its way into the crops of the baby birds.

On the sixth or seventh day, feathers, some of color, began to pierce the skin. Dickens and his nest mate passed from the ugliness of naked infancy to the ugliness of pinfeathers.

When I gently placed a finger near Dickens, the bird would raise his feathers fiercely, in the

manner of a porcupine, rear up, open his beak
wide, and snap the points together with a sharp
cracking sound that was quite frightening.

"He wants to fight, Da," I cried out in delight.

"There's heart and spirit in him," Da
agreed. "He means to defend his home. He's
learning to love it."

He turned his head toward the house, then,
as though he'd heard himself called. He smiled
wryly. My mind was on other things.

Dickens may have been learning the ways
of pigeon affection. If so, he soon took it for
granted. He apparently assumed that any
pigeon passing by should feed him, as he begged
food indiscriminately from one and all. The
rebuffs he received taught him other facts of life
and reality. He soon learned that in order to get
what he wanted and needed he'd have to do
more than shout for it. He began picking up
grain in imitation of his elders and, by the fifth
week of his life, was able to fend for himself.

When he was no longer a squab he'd become a "squeaker," peeping in a loud voice for
attention or when his nest mate pecked at him.
The squeaking stopped in the seventh week. By
that time his first molt had already begun.

I handled Dickens often. The bird had
grown unafraid, even seemed to welcome my
touch.

"Place his feet side by side," Da in-
structed. "Now hold them between the first and

second finger of your hand. So." He placed Dickens gently into my waiting hand.

"Now then, the wings are to be folded against his body. Easy. If he flutters, smooth his wings from front to back. Can your thumb reach so far around that it can hold the primary feathers?"

I could scarcely manage that, but Da pretended that I accomplished it very well while holding on himself.

"Now," he continued, "place your other hand beneath his breast. Just so, just so."

He smiled down at me as I attentively followed the simple instructions. He taught my hands even as the bird was being taught their touch.

"A bird's to be held firmly, but gently, considering its comfort, the way you should hold love or even life," Da said. And again he lifted his head, as though responding to his name, and smiled in that strange way that closed me out from memories and affairs I couldn't understand.

It was only long after I was grown, when my father and I could speak of certain things as equals, more or less, that I came to understand such smiles and other expressions that sometimes lay upon my grandfather's face.

The very lines that were spoken between us are printed on my memory, but I didn't understand certain small ironies. Nothing hidden or dramatic; such excesses were never part of our lives. It's just that I think Da smiled in that way when he spoke of love of home, and turned his head as though he were called, because he reckoned my grandmother, had she been alive to hear him spouting such pious homilies, would have taken a broom to him.

My father told me that he'd been told by his mother, Jenny, that his father had been terribly hard to tie down. He'd liked the wandering ways of a salesman.

The firm he worked for was large enough to cover New England and the eastern seaboard but not so large that it needed more than one representative, so Henri Baudoum had it all, moving his base every month or so from one territory to another. He met Jenny Austen in Rochester, courted her powerfully, in only seven meetings over the space of a year, and married her in 1894 when he was thirty-two and she nineteen. He placed her in this boarding house or that hotel and went off selling his fonts of Garamond Bold and Italic Lightface, having the best of both worlds, that of the securely married man and a footloose, fancy-free fellow as well.

Jenny never made an issue of it. She did complain softly, from time to time, of the dreary succession of strange bedrooms in shabby surroundings, but when Henri insisted that there was no reason for her to choose the cheapest establishments she simply smiled and tucked the savings away in a little painted tin souvenir box from the 1876 Philadelphia World Exhibition.

She stopped complaining altogether after the birth of Amelie. When they moved, she'd pack up the child's things with her own without complaint. She counted as furniture and possessions a rocking chair, a sewing basket, a quilt and some linens, some bits of china, a mirror, and a picture album. The infant had a doll.

She continued quiet after the birth of my father two years later. They moved seven times in the next three years, until the last child, a daughter, Agethe, came along. Then she'd had enough. She demanded a home and showed the money she'd saved for a down payment on one.

At least that's the way my grandmother told the story to my father. Admittedly, Da told one that was similar to time and circumstance but far different as far as the way it turned out. He took the position that *his* had been the dream for a house and *his* the steady, patient design of its acquisition.

Whatever the truth of it, that was a turning point in their lives.

The saltbox wasn't new, but it was solidly built. It had a porch that surrounded it and three entrances, the front, the side for tradesmen, and the one into the mud room from the backyard. There were dormer windows on the second floor and a chimney of red brick. The river was running broad and deep a long way down a gentle slope in the fold of the valley.

The house stood a short way from a stream that served it. Songbirds gathered among some willows and cottonwoods.

An old shack, more than a tool shed but less than a barn, was off to the northeast, midway between the house and stream. Chickens could be raised there if the owners were of a mind.

That's the way my father remembered it. Memories are like layers of wallpaper on a room, tear one away and the room is transformed though still essentially the same. Many people can live in it, only changing the paper.

I bend off to the side and peer around the loft house hoping to see the rushing water of the stream and the river beyond it. Not there. Memory's not quite that powerful unless one closes one's eyes. I close mine.

# *Six*

I sat in the hospital room feeling lost and uncomfortable. My father stood at the window looking into the dark street and the little park beyond it, puddled, here and there, with circles of light from the street lamps.

My mother sat beside Da's bed, smiling in the soft way she had that always made me wonder which side of the pillow her dreams lay, for all the fact that she seemed in command of things. She had her head tilted a trifle and was looking into the old man's sleeping face.

Two days and a night of strangeness and fear had gone by. I wasn't used to such solemn matters. Illness wasn't common with the Baudoums. I struggled through every minute with the feeling that a piece of my heart was caught in my throat.

My grandfather's eyes were closed, his breathing labored, his face distant as though seen through a distorting veil. Great rushing sounds came from his mouth, the gums naked as a baby's, a good deal of his dignity taken away with his false dentures. He breathed as though the air had weight. That it was a substance to be bitten and chewed.

Tears came to my eyes. I felt sorry for my grandfather. But I felt even sorrier for myself. With Da lying in the strange bed, in such unnatural sleep, I felt bitterly lonely. I was angry with him for frightening me so with this evidence of human mortality. It was too soon for my Da to go away. My grandfather had given me Dickens as my special bird and now he was leaving me alone before the race had even begun. When my *own* race had barely begun. I feared I'd get lost in the world without my grandfather. Or, if lost and then found again, deprived of Da's wise, silent understanding of the great courage I'd exercised on my journey back.

I'd been lost before.

We'd gone, my mother and father, myself and Da, to visit Aunt Tassy, Jenny's older sister, who was in her eighties when I was nine.

She lived with a companion nearly her own age, a maiden lady like herself, who was hard of hearing and smoked endless cigarettes right to the very end, nursing the last few puffs at risk of burnt lips by holding the butt end with a hairpin. Her name was Charlotte. Between the two of them, they kept Aunt Tassy's house reasonably clean but far from neat. There was an unpleasant smell as often surrounds the very old; it was even a little frightening to me.

I couldn't know the reasons for my unease but felt it strongly. I couldn't bear to be trapped in the parlor with its dusty furniture and drawn curtains. The long afternoon of reminiscences, display of old photographs kept in moldering albums, warm buttermilk forced upon me and drunk so as not to hurt the feelings of the old ladies was a delicate torture to me.

I was aware that my father suffered the day impatiently as well; regarded it as a duty to be performed from time to time, in the name of family charity. My mother didn't seem to mind. In fact seemed to enjoy it as Da seemed to do. But, then, Mother was much given to family and my grandfather to tales of youth that might be shared more easily with Tassy and her housemate because they had the years to match his own.

I bore the little pats and touchings, the buttermilk, and the heavy smell of old dust for a time, the measure of which was in my mother's keeping. When she thought it right, she'd excuse me to go out to play in the backyard, which was overgrown and tangled with wild blackberry and honeysuckle.

The old house was nearly at the edge of the little town of Helms, about twenty miles outside of Rochester. Beyond the house and yard were very few dwellings or buildings of any sort. The road and sidewalks ran out no more than half a mile away, brought to an end in the face of an area known as the South Mountain

Reservation, not quite a county park or game preserve, but something much more than a picnic ground.

A small reservoir served part of the surrounding area's water needs. A full-grown wood, laced with shadowed paths, surrounded the lake on three sides. The county road marked the fourth.

Da and I had often walked the woodland tracks and trails together in every season of the year, my grandfather pointing out the trees and flowering shrubs that he knew: canoe birch, a first messenger of autumn with its yellow leaves, the red maple and downy serviceberry flaming in the first week of the season. There was pepperidge, white oak, amur maple, and the common horse chestnut with its dark brown nuts from which Da fashioned rings for me to wear upon my fingers.

Once we came upon a fringe tree, sometimes called old-man's-beard, in a summer glade. It was only after seeing it that Da discovered what it was from a book of such lore. The first time we saw it flowering in great clusters of white blossoms hanging from the branches we thought it quite magical and pretended to believe—or did believe—that it was a wonder available only to ourselves. Once, returning to it in mid-spring, it looked dead. That's the nature of the tree. I cried. In early summer it was richly flowered and foliaged again. I learned a small lesson about life, death, and resurrection.

It was on a day in October that I went out
beyond the backyard and walked the road into
the wood, certain that I knew its paths and by-
ways. I heard the birds speaking from the
sheltering trees, turned red and gold; listened
to the wind rustling the leaves, making music.
Somewhere a wind harp sang out and tinged the
day's failing light in sadness. I walked on for a
long while until I became aware that violet
shadows, fast turning purple, were lying beneath the trees. A frog called out, heralding the
coming of night, and a dusk cricket whispered
back.

I turned around to make my way back to
the road and my Aunt Tassy's house. I stopped
all at once, frozen to the spot, looking at the
trunks of the trees, the shadows, and the choice
of paths as though I'd never before been among
them. I walked down one lane and then another,
hurrying along for some distance, then turning
back in uncertainty to try another way. Panic
rose as thick as honey in my throat. My heart
was racing. I ran along the paths, kicking up
the dust with one shoe in a nervous hop. An owl
screamed out in the growing dark. I started to
run without caution, running through weeds
and brush that slashed at my ankles. I began to
sob, a frightened sound that added to my fright.

I thought I heard my grandfather call my
name. I ran faster and found myself in the
glade with the tree called old-man's-beard
standing starkly, stripped of its summer glory.

It was no landmark to me, afforded no direction. I was lost.

I stood very still, trying not to cry, waiting for the breath to still in me. When it did, I heard the soft spill of water to my right. I made my way through the underbrush, not caring about the lack of paths or the scratches I received on my hands and arms. I came to the reservoir and a spillway fashioned of logs. An inch of water poured over the edge, purling softly. Beyond were more trees. And beyond them was the sound of motorcars and their headlamps flickering through the tree trunks and limbs. The road to town.

I had to get across, but I couldn't swim and was afraid. Afraid of wetting and spoiling my shoes even if I made it across without mishap. Afraid of drowning all alone. I thought awhile and could see no other way. I put my courage to the test.

Bending over and placing my hands on the logs below the thin surface of the water, I walked four-footed across the span, all fifty yards of it, and made the opposite shore.

When I was back at Aunt Tassy's at last, I found the grown-ups still sitting in the parlor, telling stories, lost in a spell of old time. I'd scarcely been missed. My mother looked at me and smiled.

My father said, "There you are. We're going now. Say good-bye to Aunt Tassy and Miss Charlotte."

"Where'd you get those scratches, in the

berry patch?" Aunt Tassy said. "Should clear it out. Doesn't bear much fruit anymore. Getting old."

In the car driving back to Rochester I sat in the back with my grandfather, wanting to tell someone about my adventure but afraid of the scolding that might follow. Still, I'd acted bravely and I wanted someone to know of it even if my foolishness had to be revealed.

I felt my grandfather's hand on my knee. I turned my head to see Da looking at my shoes. Da smiled into my eyes.

"Were you lost, then?" he asked, putting his mouth close to my ear and whispering.

"Yes, Da. By the spillway," I said, doing the same.

"You walked across?"

"Yes. I was afraid," I confided.

"Afraid of being lost or walking the logs?"

"Both. Of everything in the dark."

My grandfather put pressure on my leg, a man's compliment. "Bravely done," he said.

I must have sobbed at the memory because my mother looked at me swiftly, measuring my control. I wiped at my eyes with the heel of my hand. It was a little boy's gesture and I was immediately sorry for it. I hoped she wouldn't come over to comfort me. That would surely make me break down and cry like a baby. I lifted my chin, looked at her and tried a small smile which, happily, didn't slide off my face. My mother nodded and turned back to her quiet, mysterious contemplation of Da's old face.

Da's eyes opened. They were filled with the most terrible fear and confusion for a moment. They cast about the room seeking something. They fell on me with such urgency in their expression that I stood up as though called.

Da managed to raise his right hand and arm a trifle and no more, but it seemed to beckon me.

My mother bent over Da. She tried to lift him and settle him more comfortably upon the pillows. My father turned from the window and moved to help. Da's eyes snapped. As sunken and collapsed as he seemed in the bed, his spirit was strong and insistent. Mother and Father seemed to understand that they were to stop their fussing over him. At least my mother said, "All right, Pa," and moved away.

Da turned his eyes to me again and I went to the bed and took my grandfather's hand. It felt weak and loose, the way his face looked, all sagging and drawn to one side like the mask of a melting wax figure. The eye on the left teared badly, overrunning the dark pink well of the lower lid like water from a tilted saucer. I took a tissue from the box on the bedside table and gently wiped my grandfather's tears from his cheek. Da tried to smile at me. It was a terrible effort that made me want to cry out that he shouldn't try such expressions of thanks.

Da opened his mouth to speak. Slobber ran from his mouth to his chin and I wiped that away as well. He tried to speak again. It was scarcely human, an animal's attempt to communicate, rough and painful to hear.

"The race starts in the morning, Hugh. Dickens will win." At least that's what I think Da wanted to say, though it sounded nothing like it.

But I seemed to understand, so closely had our minds and hearts become tuned to one another. The words all turned round by the stroke, syllables askew, were more a communication heart to heart than tongue to ear.

I nodded and gripped my grandfather's hand, trying to tell him that I'd be watchful for Dickens's triumph over time and distance. That I'd be watching his own struggle to win back to health and home.

"I'll be up with the sun, Da," I said. "I'll come tell you the time the birds went off, the weather and all, as soon as I know."

I'm trying to shape a picture of my grandfather. Not only what I remember of him, the love we shared, the mystery and pain of that fateful day and the days that followed, but the total substance of him as I came to know him through stories and little secrets told about him when he was gone and I was grown.

A small boy may see a saint in his grandfather, as I did, but a man seeks other means to know the man who, in his great age, reached down to childhood and helped me grow.

I don't know exactly how this particular story I'm about to relate came to my attention. I'm sure my father didn't tell me of it; I doubt he would have approved of anyone knowing. Perhaps my mother told me, for, though it showed my grandfather to be somewhat sinful, it also showed him most human, and my mother would understand the dearness of that.

It seems that my grandfather, grown restless at his job, had accepted the offer of another which would have required a move to New York City. It was to be a position as typesetter and linotype operator with a city newspaper. A step up, he said, and an end to his gypsy ways. A similar offer had been made to him right in Rochester, and Grandmother knew it, but he'd refused it as being too small an arena for his temperament.

He might have been discontent with the nest he found her folding around him, but she'd settled into the little house by the stream like a bird. It made a quarrel between them. Both were stubborn and, in the end, Da went off to Manhattan alone. They were separated, then, by nearly the width of the state, almost two hundred miles as the crow flies. Far too far back in 1903 or 1904 to be trotting home every weekend. He did come home, of course, from time to time.

I'm a gadling, I suppose, much like Da had been, but, unlike him, I've never lost the habit. Where once he'd chafed at being surrounded by too much comfort, he clearly came to savor it. Jenny bought him a great, soft Morris chair as a birthday surprise and that might well have been the final nail in his domestication. He'd tell me how he'd sit in it, paper in hand to be read between dozings. I know the feeling and fly from it.

Da told me, too, that they played word games way back then. There'd been no television or even radio. They did have an early phonograph and listened to Enrico Caruso on it.

In the night, I wonder, did he lie awake feeling his wife's body along the length of his back and thighs, and did her familiar body seem strange because of their separations? Was he reminded of strange bodies that had become familiar even in their variety? How did she feel? Had she ever come close to telling him that he needn't come home at all?

Something happened, and this is the scene I can only piece together from what was told me or what I simply surmise.

There was a lady—a "sob-sister" she was called—who worked on the newspaper Da worked for. The *Herald* I believe. She started out to be a friend, then a drinking companion. She was dead-ended because of her sex, relegated to the fashion page, women's page, little stories of human heart-throb designed to bring tears and sell papers. He'd lost out on some of his own dreams. He was no poet, but perhaps she thought he was—or could be.

I imagine they got on well together, feeding each other's hopes, bolstering each other's egos.

Pretending in one another's company that they would find their way, someday, to that special fate or fame awaiting them. She'd come to think that fate was meant for both of them together. I suppose she pressed marriage on him. Had he resisted? Had she lowered her expectations and agreed to simply live with him? Did he consider the possibility of having, without a second marriage but in practical fact, two wives, two households, and, probably soon enough, two sets of children? It's happened. Did he love the woman? Did she love him?

I'm not sure that really matters. What matters is that he went home to put the virtues of those two lives side by side. It was a time of decision and, according to whoever told the tale to me, Jenny knew it.

She'd challenged him right off.

"So one of the cats you've teased has scratched you," Jenny'd said clearly in the dark.

"What?" he'd probably shouted in sheer startlement.

"Don't you understand me, Henri?"

"Well, you'll have to speak clearer than that," he'd stammered.

"I thought you writers enjoyed a good metaphor," Jenny said. She reached out, turned on the bedside lamp, and arranged herself against the pillows, covers to her collarbones, prepared to adjudicate his case.

He remained lying as he was, back turned to her.

"I think you'd best sit up and look this matter squarely in the eye, Henri. I have for some long time."

He did as he was told.

"I meant to say," Jenny went on, "that you've had your women——"

"I would like——" he interrupted.

"Don't," Jenny interrupted in her turn. "I don't want you to protest your innocence. Neither am I going to say that I understand a man's need for a woman 'just for the sake of his health.' I don't think you'd buy my taking lovers for the sake of mine. You've had your pleasure."

"I never deprived you or the children of anything in order to satisfy any appetite of mine."

"Do be quiet, Henri," Jenny said, almost sharply. "I'm trying to sort this out for both of us. I expect you would support your children. They're as much yours as mine. Of that you can be sure," she added significantly. "So I won't be pinning any roses on you for acting in good faith in circumstances which you created.

"Up to now your affairs have been casual. That's been clear to me."

"Didn't you mind?" Henri asked, somehow offended.

"Very much. But I'd handed you an ultimatum. I'd refused to go with you because I wanted this home. I intended to be as fair as I knew how to be."

"More than fair," he murmured unhappily.

"I think so, yes," she agreed. "That's so much water over the bridge."

"Over the dam," he said absently.

"Whichever," Jenny agreed with no sign of her annoyance. "But it's clear to me that one of your ladies is asking for more than your night-time company."

"How do you know that?"

"Is it true?"

"Yes, but how do you know?"

Jenny smiled softly. "My skin tells me things, Henri. You know you ought to listen to your skin."

"What do you mean?"

"Well," she said and thought awhile, choosing her comparisons.

"Does your skin feel good when you walk down by the river through the mist?"

"It does."

"Better than the alleys and streets of New York?"

"Much."

"Does your skin feel good on Sunday afternoon when you've had your dinner and you're sitting in your chair by the fire on a winter's afternoon?"

He nodded, eyes misting up like a man being told about things in which he'd lost the right to partake.

"How does it feel when you put on freshly washed pajamas and slip between freshly laundered and ironed sheets?"

"Goddam wonderful," Henri blurted out, about to cry.

"Better than the sheets changed when the thought comes into a chambermaid's head?"

"Much."

"You'll sleep in your underwear back there, won't you?"

Henri nodded his head, much ashamed of such slovenly habits.

"That's what I mean about listening to your skin."

He was thoughtful for a long while. He looked at her dear face, hair long and loose and heavy along her shoulders. She looked back at him calm and composed, having had her say, prepared to forgive him, he knew, but not prepared to accept any prolongation of his tomcat ways or wayward existence.

"Can I try an experiment?" he said.

"Tell me what it is."

He unbuttoned his pajama top and took it off. Jenny lowered the bodice of her nightgown. They came together, skin to skin.

"I'm coming home," he'd said.

At least that's the way I imagine it may have been, sitting here with the sun slipping down the sky.

# *Seven*

The early part of the night spent in Hillsboro was filled with an excitement of anticipation for Dickens. The long, scattered hours of the journey were over and he sensed that the moment of release was nearly due.

All the grain was removed from the feeders in the baskets. No trainers wanted their birds flown with heavy crops. Tests and observations had proved that there was no special energy value in feeding soon before a race. It'd been discovered that digestion slowed down, almost stopped, during the rigors of flight. Full crops meant only extra weight. Water, however, was left in the cups with bits of sponge so that, if the water was spilled during the night, the sponges would hold enough to keep the birds refreshed.

Dickens sat on the dowel roost in the basket without anxiety or nervousness. Even his excitement finally died in the deep of night and he slept as pigeons sleep, with eyes open.

At first light a new sense of expectancy

aroused them all. An electricity of competition passed among them. They shifted about within the confines of the baskets, tried their wings, murmured and muttered to themselves, wanting to be off and flying in the morning air.

Dickens was in prime condition. Not one tail or flight feather was missing or broken. His plumage was oily, silky to the touch. A white bloom was on it.

Just under the skin upon the keelbone a little clot of blood pulsated, the notable mark of a bird in the very top of its form. Dickens was a champion trained and tuned to the moment.

The race committee of the Hillsboro Racing Pigeon Union walked the line of benches as the baskets were set out by other members. The selected men from Rochester, who'd traveled with the birds, walked along with them.

The sun rose above a distant stand of trees, feathering the edges of the massed leaves in cool light. A solar breeze swept across the land. It was sweet to the tongue and freshened the minds of birds and men alike.

The baskets were opened, the birds released into the luminous morning. The time was marked by the hands of a "perfect" clock. Four hundred and twenty-six birds rushed into the sky. They climbed above the height of the tallest tree and formed into kits.

When pigeons fly, they seek the company of others of their kind. This attraction is powerful and natural. The trainer must find ways to break his birds of the habit, for a fast bird is often caught up by the flock pull, and time is wasted. Some remain with a kit of slower birds all the way and lose races they might have won with ease if flown alone.

The ideal bird finds the heights, ignores the flock and kits, takes its bearings, and chooses the most direct air-line to home. Dickens was one of these. He soared high above the other birds, climbing like a dart. With powerful beats of his wings, an air of exaltation, he answered the demands of his will to go home. He raced toward Rochester. All the training and purpose of his life had come together in the driving moment.

Dickens had been early bred so his training hadn't begun until he was nearly into his eighth week.

I'd held Dickens so that his head faced my forearm, settled in my hand without cramping or undue restraint. Da carried the nest mate, Scrooge, named for the habit it had of squinting up its eyes in mean and doubtful contemplation.

Three wicker baskets filled with other young birds were lined up on the bed of my red wagon. We were off on the first training flight only a short walk away, about five blocks to the empty lot on the corner of Peach and Waverly.

Da's trips were well known along the route, a mark of early summer as dependable as the flowering of the fringe trees and dogwoods I do suppose.

"This," Da said, as we strolled along, holding our pets and pulling the wagon behind us, "is the beginning of Dickens's responsibility to himself."

"What do you mean, Da?"

"Well, he's had nothing but his freedom. That's a good thing to have, but some creatures —some people—don't really know what it is."

"What is it?"

"What do you think?" Da asked.

I thought about it for the length of a dozen strides.

"Now don't go dwelling on it and saying what you think is proper or pleasing, Hugh. Say right out."

"Freedom's to do what you want?"

"Any time?"

"I think."

"As long as you please?"

I nodded.

"Without caring?"

"Caring about what?"

"Making your bread, earning your keep, doing those things you've been set to do in company with other people."

"Chores? You mean chores, Da?"

"Keeping and caring," Da nodded. "Doing what you've been given to do when you're able. Making your own way."

"I'm too small yet to make my own way, Da," I said.

"Indeed, but small as he is, Dickens runs on

pigeon time and he's to be taught something of freedom now.''

"We want him to fly to the loft, don't we?'' I cried out, suddenly afraid that I would lose my pet. "You don't expect him to fly away and leave?''

"It could happen—has happened—but I think not. We've made him comfortable. He knows your touch. But even if we knew that he'd fly away forever we'd have to test his will to come home all the same. It's one mark of freedom. A creature returns to home for the good that's in it. For the caring and the rightness. Every creature has to be given the right to chase the far reaches of the sky, find the limits and accept them gracefully. Frogs make foolish bulls no matter how much they huff and puff and swell themselves up.''

"Did you look for the reaches of the sky, Da?'' I asked.

He smiled softly and looked off with his sailor's eyes. His voice was soft and graveled with emotion. He spoke to somebody else, not me. Somebody who wasn't really there.

"Fifty is a trying time for men. Young women call you 'sir' and kiss you on the corner of the mouth but don't try to linger there. They sometimes hug you for a while longer than they should. But it's as though it's for the young man that you were.''

"Women are like that,'' I said, thinking of Aunt Tassy and her friend, besides any number of other female relatives and acquaintances who had a habit of holding me close till I feared I'd smother against their bosoms. I was pretty clear about what Da meant.

He smiled down on me.

"Yes, well," he said. "Bothersome creatures they are.

"You'd never believe it at the moment but there'll come a time when the loss of such pleasures, and others that you'll learn about in time, leaves you feeling kind of sad. Makes you feel some joy has gone from life. Wakes the gadling in a man."

"Did you want to fly off to the reaches of the sky again?"

"Indeed. I was fifty-three and fighting the sadness that half a century had laid on me, your aunts married and gone away, your pa new married and set up in a house of his own. I had my work, of course. But the house was gloomy Saturday afternoons and Sundays. There was nothing much for me to do. Your grandmother had a nest box made and gave me a pair of pigeons for occupation."

"That was nice."

"I suppose, but I resented it. I took a leave from the newspaper. I had one more try at the other side of the mountain."

"But you came back."

"Lickety-split. My bones were aching from sleeping rough on the ground or in strange beds. It wasn't for me anymore. I was domesticated and loved my nest. I was like a pigeon, free to fly away but content to stay at home. I tried to leave. That's how come I can talk so foolish and so certain about such things.''

We reached the grassy lot, knee high to Da, nearly waist high on me. It was filled with green foxtail, curly dock, and quack grass. Here and there red sorrel sent up its crimson spikes, oxeye daisy made pretty and dandelion blossomed butter-gold. Little gnats and tiny moths whirled about in the pollen dust kicked up by our passage.

In the center of the small field the baskets were opened and the birds released. Dickens and Scrooge were tossed from our hands. They joined together in a flock, just a touch confused and edgy, chattering among themselves concerning their whereabouts until one or another got the right of it and started back to the loft.

''There they go,'' Da said, ''like a bunch of noisy kids going home from school. Wanting company all the way. We'll be changing that.''

We walked back to the loft, rested awhile and handled the birds, then put them in the baskets again for another walk back to the corner of Peach and Waverly.

The second time we tossed the birds individually, five minutes apart, so they wouldn't kit up and wait for other birds before making for the loft.

The following morning we'd walked out about a mile to the top of a hill, sent the birds off all together, then one at a time as before, lengthening the distance of flight, trusting to the love of loft and nest bred into the birds to see them safely home. We walked a lot those years.

Now Da lay trapped in a body that would not respond to his will. He was incontinent from time to time. I wonder what terrible humiliation that must have been to him. I'd sometimes overheard him speaking of death with older men, with Fouquet and others of his age. They'd all come to some bargain with the inevitability of it. They talked at length only about the manner of it; which deaths were preferable. All agreed that they feared any disease or dysfunction that would strip from them the means to stand in the presence of the Reaper, composed if not entirely unafraid. It seemed to me to be morbid talk, vaguely shivery like a witch's tale. When Da saw me listening in, he'd quickly turn the subject away, not because he thought children shouldn't know of death but because he didn't choose to have me know that he was so much concerned by the prospect of it.

I'm certain that the efficient and casual way in which he was handled in the hospital terrified and enraged him.

He was as helpless as a baby, unable to make his wants known except by the most exhausting effort of will. He was then accused of being difficult; of resisting all the good they wished to do him. At times he was discussed by the professionals as though he couldn't hear, an infant to be managed instead of a grown man to be consulted.

I'm sure he concentrated on the world available to him, trying to define that much of it which he could hope to control in some way. Anything outside the hospital was out of reach. Indeed, anything outside the room in which he was imprisoned went on its way without heed of him, except for a portion of the sky.

I'd propped his head on the pillows to one side so that he might take what hope or joy he could from the reaches of the sky. I was deeply involved in an act of loving, uncaring of practical concerns. I'd intuited that Da wanted at least that much of freedom. I gave him the small public park on the other side of the broad road that led to the hospital. From his angle of view Da could see a kite soaring below the clouds; could follow the string along its bellied path toward the earth but probably couldn't see below the sill to the end of it. Did he wonder who held it tethered to the ground?

Without a human being, visible and real, Da hadn't much trust in things standing alone as marks or symbols. Things had no existence as far as my grandfather was concerned, despite the fact that his poet's consciousness often dealt with myth and metaphor. He often spoke to me in parables. I think he felt himself, without undue conceit, a philosopher in the mold of Robert Frost or Carl Sandburg, simple, homely, and unpretentious. The little verses he sometimes composed for me spoke of landscapes but sang of barns and fences as well, objects touched by the hand of man.

He told me once of coming home that last time, an aging boy, a weary gadling, hungry for the nest. He'd waited till he was alone, Jenny gone to quietly prepare a homecoming meal, before walking around the little house beside the river touching things, making them real. The rocking chair, a table beside a wingback, another by the fire displaying small bits of china in the shapes of dogs and cats, the very floors and walls.

Bird talk murmured up on the river breezes. He went out into the yard and walked down to the shed, a shed no more.

It had been painted white, its roof tiled in blue. A small steeple had been added to it topped by a weathervane of three birds in silhouette rising from a marshland. There were a dozen pigeons or more strutting and pouting about on a small porch before the nest box doors.

Jenny came down to stand with him.

"Pretty, aren't they," she'd said.

"I thought you were fondest of your singing canary," Da'd replied.

"Petey can't be let out of the cage. These birds can and must be set free from time to time. But they rarely fly off and not come home."

"Are you telling me something?"

She'd kissed him on his cheek and laughed. The laughter—Da said—was very young and very wise.

When I came into the room at my grandfather's back, a sound burst from his lips that sounded to me like a cry of anguish. I ran around to the other side of the bed, looked into his face and saw with relief that he was really trying to laugh at some happy thought. I laughed a little too.

"Watching the kite, Da?" I asked.

He raised his right hand a little and clucked softly in his throat. Bird talk.

"I understand, Da," I said. "The birds were tossed at half past six this morning. The winds were light and southeasterly in a clear sky."

Da said, "It won't be long now and you'll have yourself a Concourse winner."

It didn't come out that way. Not at all. It came out a long series of garbled syllables, evil-sounding and ugly. Even as he tried to speak, Da tried to call back the sounds. I suppose he saw a subtle look of shock and pain on my face, though I tried to hide it. But the spate of his words wouldn't be stemmed; his tongue ran on uncontrolled, trying of its own volition to complete the thought and make itself understood, a treasonous organ of speech running wild and humiliating him. He closed his eyes against the shame of it.

I grabbed his hand hard and went down on my knees beside the bed.

"Oh, Da," I said, "you just got to stay with me. You just can't go away and get lost."

Da made a choking sound that rose into

his mouth. He opened his eyes again and peered into my face.

"You have to be here for the end of the race," I said as though this was a proper bargain to be struck with God.

God's world went on.

Last year's leaves, uncovered by the warm, thawing days of spring, dried out, fragile as tissue paper, light as floss, were swept up from the streets of Sault Sainte Marie in Michigan, from the glades and forests surrounding, and deposited into the Soo Canals.

The winds blew moderate to fresh, twelve to twenty miles an hour, gusting occasionally. They gave a pleasant spice to the air, a hint of rain. White clouds rolled high above. The winds danced across Lake Huron on the way to meet a chill mass of polar air moving down from the north.

In another part of the sky a peregrine falcon sailed at one thousand feet above the valley of the Wabash just south of Terre Haute, Indiana. She and the tercel that was her mate defended a territory of nearly eight square miles across the gently rolling hills, river bottom, and thick stands of poplar dotted here and there. She soared up on the rising thermals, altering the pitch of her wings to ride the winds.

Migrant birds, passerines of all sorts, would have done well to cross her domain when she was on the nest, perched after satiating herself upon a kill or preening in the quiet hours of the day. Once aloft and on the hunt, noiselessly riding the reaches of the sky, she was a terror. She examined every foot of the width and length and depth of her nation, alert for prey.

After two hours of flight from the beginning of the race, Dickens entered her kingdom.

The sun is lowering in the sky, just disappearing beyond the apartment block, and a breeze with some hint of chill in it seems to rise immediately from the land.

The reverie that fills me, the fragmented thoughts that occupy my mind, dashing me back and forth across the years as though I had no will of my own, is a rich tapestry. I can feel myself a six-year-old boy again with my very first pigeon that was my own and no other's under my hands, an older boy of ten suffering the helplessness I felt before my grandfather's terrible illness, a youth of fourteen at the funeral of a woman who had a blue glass eye. All of these and more. A different youth, young man, adult for each of the years of my life. At least for every one of the small epochs that attend our journey there to here—to somewhere.

I am suddenly shaken by a terrible regret that I had no children and, because of that, lack a grandchild—preferably a boy—with whom I might share my thoughts and feelings as once Da shared them with me. Not because it would be expected that grown-up concerns would be understood or remedies to trouble advised, but simply because it would be flesh of my flesh listening to the sad song of life's passage that is so much sadder when there is no flesh of one's flesh to listen.

I'm certain that my grandfather must have looked upon me as a small bundle of his own blood and bone more than half a century removed, himself reborn to wonder at the marvels of the world, my eyes his, my ears his, my tongue upon the first sweet apple his as well. I must have seemed to him a solemn repository of Henri Baudoum's better tales, verses, fables; his wisdom and hard-earned knowledge. A well that he was filling even if it did not completely understand, and that would, in good time, give it back to another Baudoum along the line. I've failed him in that regard, but not in the sharpness of my recall which is its own special dedication and tribute.

# Eight

The diagnosis of stroke is not a simple matter. In a man of my grandfather's age it was extremely complicated. The symptoms he displayed might have been the consequences of tumor, abscess, shrinkage of the brain from a hundred causes, encephalitis, epilepsy, meningitis, and complications of such ailments as diabetes or a dozen toxic states. Da had never held much with doctors or regular examinations, had always enjoyed good health, and so there wasn't much on record, except the obvious evidence of age, to help the doctor in his final conclusion. It was, of course, finally achieved.

"We can definitely identify the stroke as a carotid thrombosis," Dr. Sand had said. His voice had been pitched professionally low and his back, as he faced my mother and father in the far corner of the hospital room, was turned toward Da who lay in bed, apparently asleep, unaware of the sun on his face or of me standing by his bedside.

My father cleared his throat nervously as

though embarrassed to admit ignorance of the technical expressions used. Dr. Sand touched his arm and smiled apologetically.

"I'm sorry. That doesn't mean a thing to you. There are several kinds of physical insults all grouped under the general layman's term 'stroke.' In your father's case he showed indications of two types, but now we've pinned it down."

He half turned toward the bed as though checking to make certain Da wasn't listening in on the conversation that was about him. It was an automatic gesture, the sort a doctor makes who's busy, on the run, doing service for relatives, as well as patients, fitting things in.

"His paralysis isn't limited to only one side of the body. That's unusual but can be explained by a half dozen factors."

"But he can raise his right hand," my father said.

Dr. Sand smiled as though commending him on finding the hopeful sign.

"The dominant side of his brain has been damaged more than the other. That's why there's a disruption in the reception and expression of speech."

My mother sighed deeply. "Will he be all right?" she said and then ducked her head in recognition of the simplicity and inadequacy of the remark, the foolishness of it.

"Not 'all right,' but we can hope for improvement since he's survived these first hours," Dr. Sand assured her. "There is, of course, the possibility of another incident."

The three of them seemed to contemplate that terrible threat.

"What's to be done?" she asked.

"He'll stay here, of course, until his condition is reasonably stable. We'll have to consult a rehabilitation team."

"Oh?" she said.

"That would be a physical therapist, occupational therapist—"

"Da keeps himself busy. Nobody has to find things for him to do," my mother said.

Dr. Sand smiled briefly and went on. "Speech therapist—"

"Oh yes."

"Psychologist—"

My father shuffled his feet. A small frown appeared between his brows. Get on with it, he seemed to say.

"Social worker," Dr. Sand went on, lost in the pattern of his own speech, unable to let it go. "Vocational counselor," he finished, running down like an old clock.

"He doesn't need a social worker," my father said. "He's got a family."

"You both work, don't you?" Dr. Sand said.

They nodded.

"Well, then, you'll be needing help of one sort or another."

"He can stay here until we work things out?" my father asked.

"Yes. We'll handle things to make it as

easy as we can all around. For now. But you understand the hospital isn't set up to take care of chronic patients."

My parents nodded again, taking things with apparent calm, listening to the doctor order the disruption of their lives, fearing the burden of an invalid not because they didn't love my grandfather who suffered, but because they recognized the human weakness in themselves and feared they'd come to begrudge the care they gave to Da when their own spirits were diminished.

Sitting by my grandfather and overhearing most of the murmured conversation, I told myself, and would have told everyone who cared to listen, that I'd take care of my grandfather. I'd stay up all day and all night if need be, holding my grandfather's hand so he wouldn't slip away. Feeding him. Bathing his strong old limbs now stricken weak and useless, cooling the fever that lay upon his skin. Just as Da had done for me when I was small and ill.

I'd contracted measles. In the night, just before the rash appeared, my temperature rose to 105 degrees. I awakened with the weight of the fever on my eyelids and saw Da sitting beside my bed in the yellow glow of the bedlamp. He was wringing out a cloth in a pan of water, the sound reminding me of the bustle of water over the stones of the brooks that led to the Genesee River. Da turned toward the bed and saw me looking at him.

"How is it, sonny?" he whispered.

"I'm thirsty."

"Well, sure you are."

Da gave me a sip of cool water, holding my head up from the pillow.

He placed the damp cloth on my forehead.

"Men of the Foreign Legion put wet cloths around their heads when marching from one oasis to another," Da said. "Keeps their brains from cooking."

"No," I laughed.

"Would I pull your leg?"

"No, but you might tickle my fancy," I said.

We laughed together softly in the room with the night outside the window. An owl spoke.

"That's not a hunter, is it, Da?" I asked, a bit concerned about the pigeons.

"Just a little hooter looking for nothing bigger than a grasshopper. Besides, our birds are all to bed."

"More water, please," I said.

I drank again and made a small sound of discomfort.

"Feeling poorly, aren't you?" Da said.

"Will I get better soon?"

I imagine Da wondered how a child feeling badly could be told the sickness he suffered was a comparatively small matter. How long was "soon" to a boy? Was it shorter than a day? Shorter even than an hour?

"How long is 'soon'?" he asked, scarcely knowing that he'd spoken aloud.

"Till morning comes," I said. Being practical in my request for miracles.

"Ah," Da smiled, "then you count the times the owl calls. When he speaks seven times the sun will be topping Wager's hill. Morning'll be on the way and you'll be feeling better."

The owl spoke again and I counted "one."

I was asleep again before seven calls were heard. That was when I was eight or nine. Now I was ten and Da was ill.

I leaned close to my grandfather's pillow and whispered into his ear.

"Listen for the owl, Da. Morning's on the way."

Dickens was beating his way through it with powerful strokes of his wings, pushing aside the sunny air. There was no weariness in him. Not the least breath. He wasn't aware of it—didn't care—but he was far ahead of every other bird in the race, even so early on. At the rate he was going he'd surely be the winner, the champion and a record setter. His urge to reach the nest blinded him somewhat to the dangerous shape hovering above him; the pointed wings and serpent's head.

But the peregrine saw him.

Dickens's entire spirit was on his mate and the young she was caring for. An engine of desire ran him. One of hunger drove the falcon. Her sharp eyes weighed and measured him.

The look of her high among the clouds was

one of great and tranquil beauty. A ripple of pure white dotted with umber from below. A silken ribbon of flight opening and closing as she angled across the sky, wings curling in the sun.

Now she gathered herself, folded her wings tight against her body, collected herself for the stoop, and came plummeting out of the sun which helped to blind Dickens to her deadly approach.

When she struck, the air would be filled with his feathers, the wreckage of his defeat. She'd ride him down for a distance, then let him go to fall, stunned, to the boscage and brier below. Then she would alight upon him, instinctively mantling him with spread wings in order to conceal her kill from any other predators. She would break his neck with a powerful wrench and, finally, feed upon him.

Her body, hurtling down, obscured an infinitesimal spot of the sun, shadowed Dickens's back for a split moment, cooled it an imperceptible fraction of a degree but warned him nonetheless.

The falcon's eyes were placed well forward for the benefit such vision gave to attacking creatures of prey, his well to the side for the virtue that extended peripheral vision gave to those who depended upon alertness and flight to preserve their lives. He saw the shape of her bringing death. Her talons were outstretched and hooked to destroy. He paused in mid-flight, fell away from the direct line of his flight, turned aside.

The falcon shot by, striking him a glancing blow with her compact body. He chattered across the sky, momentarily out of control. But he wasn't wounded, not even stunned. Only terrified and running for his life.

She hurtled on, nearly bombing into the ground, curling back her powerful flight feathers with a turn of her wrists, warping and bellying her wings at the last moment. She seemed to collide with a wall of air and bounced back into the sky, having stopped mere inches from the killing earth.

Dickens raced away in stark terror and confusion, employing no tactics, simply flying on in the vain hope that the peregrine, having struck, would strike no more.

The peregrine flamed away from the brown earth, the rocks greened with moss and lichen that lay in the swampy bogs along the banks of the Wabash, the patches of new grass, bright green, unstained. She thrust herself toward the sun that had somehow betrayed her to her prey. She beat against the pull of the earth and climbed the columns of the sky, tier upon tier, until she was at a thousand feet again, turning about on planing wings, effortlessly gliding upon the updrafts as she searched the altitudes below.

There was her quarry—there was Dickens —beating his way furiously, but stupidly, on a straight line, away from the shelter of the stands of trees dotted here and there upon the landscape, heading out into the most open of the ground.

She leaned back onto the air and set herself to stoop once more. She hurtled down. Her speed increased. She became a living stone, a feathered projectile as deadly as any made of lead or steel.

Dickens gathered his sense and his wiles. He took hold of himself and surveyed the dimensions of the danger he was in. He saw a stand of willows cradled in a small bend of the river. He half turned on his back, slowing himself so severely that he began to fall at once. He fluttered briefly to right himself, went left, then right.

The peregrine saw what he meant to do but was committed to her attack. She was able to alter her trajectory only enough so that she would still transect the new direction of the pigeon's flight. She would have him this time.

Dickens stopped again, zigged and zagged as before, then seemed to leap forward and up into the air, throwing all the peregrine's calculations awry. Still she struck him. He felt a terrible wrenching of the muscles of his left wing where they were sheathed to his breastbone and ribs. Feathers exploded into the sky. Was he pierced?

He flew on. He felt nothing broken. There was no wetness of blood, no pink spray upon the air. He felt no veil of dark vertigo before his eyes. He gained heart and strength as the stand of willow grew near.

The falcon approached the earth again, braked and pulled away, screaming and chattering her anger at the second loss of her victim.

The protection promised by the trees was still about a mile away, a minute or less for a racing pigeon in the fullness of its strength. But Dickens was hurt and slowed down considerably. He pumped his wings against the pain in his side and careened toward the trees.

The peregrine climbed again, not quite so high. If she was to take this pigeon before it gained the safety of the willows she'd have to shorten the distance of her dive. She turned and sought him out. He was lost down below amid the undergrowth and rocks for a long moment. Her own eagerness for the kill affected her usually pin-sharp sight. She had nestlings to feed.

Then she saw Dickens flying very low to the ground. Sending his shadow among the other shadows on the earth. He was gathering speed even in so short a run, apparently recovered from the glancing blow she'd dealt him. She chose a line of attack, set herself, and stooped. She pierced the sky like an arrow, her every sense centered on the moment of impact.

Dickens had no tactics or strategies left. He didn't dare to waste a moment in any diversionary movements. Straight ahead lay salvation and he needed every ounce of speed and strength to reach it. The trunks of the trees loomed closer. The texture of the bark and the details of leaves became clear. He sensed the peregrine hurtling toward him, sensed death at his back.

Then he was among the shadows cast by the trees. A last heroic effort placed him beneath their boughs. He was safe.

The falcon crashed through the foliage. She leapt away on curled wings. She flew off shouting curses at the pigeon. Dickens flew deeper into the grove where the peregrine couldn't follow. He perched on a limb and examined his sanctuary. It was a random stand, isolated in the little curve of the river, unconnected by any heavy growth or stretch of bush to the thick woods that grew back in a long line from the river edge, a windbreak planted once long ago by men who'd set out to farm the land. That was a half mile away across a space bare except for sedge and soft grasses. He'd be safer if he could make his way across that distance and wrap the weight of the greater forest around him.

The falcon seemed to have given him up as a potential meal for herself and her family, but, if she was unsuccessful upon the hunt as the day wore on, she might decide to make incursions into the small wood even if it were not her natural hunting ground. Dickens eyed the distance to the forest and saw no easy way across it. He flew to a tree on the farthest rim and perched again. He cocked his head, keeping an eye on the deadly shape quartering the sky above.

As he kept his vigil, waiting for the peregrine to make a kill or go farther afield, Dickens saw a pheasant burst from cover, flushed out by some danger greater, more immediate, than the falcon coursing the sky above. Dickens saw the slender, sinuous shape of a weasel slithering through the brush, head lifted to watch the pheasant's flight, showing its teeth in anger at the loss of its quarry.

The pheasant rose in the air, all gold, black, and russet. The falcon fell from the sky, a thunderbolt. She collided with the pheasant. Its feathers exploded in a cloud. There was a burst of crimson spray. The peregrine rode the pheasant to earth, never letting go. She broke its neck, her talons sunk deep in its breast. She mantled it with her wings.

Dickens burst from the protection of the willows, crossed the open space, and entered the wood beyond. The shadows were cool. He perched again behind a veil of pine needles and waited to regain his strength.

He was alive, the pheasant dead. He rested gratefully.

I don't believe there was any good rest for my grandfather that second terrible day. We left him at last—life's chores had to be attended—alone to the white room and the fading sun lying heavy on the windowsill. It seemed to have weight to me as it spilled over the edge onto the floor. I wondered if Da thought it so.

Or did he think, instead, of the terrible weight of the stroke that gripped him. Or perhaps, the last lingering illness that took my grandmother from him.

I remember now being told of how hard he'd fought to hold her to life. My mother said once to me that Da "had woven a garment out of willpower, so often patched and mended that it was no more than a beggar's rag, and with it wrapped his Jenny safe as long as he could."

She told me of my grandmother lying in the little bedroom within sight of the river and sound of the pigeons cooing in the dusk. It was only then the shades were raised, the curtains opened, for the light of day hurt her eyes. Or perhaps she knew that it illuminated too harshly for her Henri's eyes to bear the ravages of her flesh.

But for a little while in the violet shadows of twilight they could look out upon the familiar landscape and, in the lovely light of waning day, it was not so apparent that her body was thinned to a pity or that her hands had seemed to grow large and ungainly as she became diminished.

It was then that my Da would hold her and whisper into her hair, his dry lips softly stirring grandmother's hair, fine now, gossamer, no longer thick and heavy as she lay against his breast.

So my mother came upon them more than once and, upon one occasion, heard Da softly putting iron in Grandma's spirit with promises that he would hold her in the last moments of her life and a little longer after.

The gloaming is falling on the land.

# Nine

Dickens wanted to fly out from under the cover of the sheltering trees but a large fear still stayed with him. He shivered as though taken with a chill despite the fact that the heat of the afternoon had been held in the forest. Warm breezes swept along the earth between river and trees, kicking up dust devils, joining with the lengthening shadows to produce a clinging damp, fragile and shifting.

He rose from the branch, lifting his wings, and cried out in anguish. The roosting had restored something of his strength but had allowed a stiffening of his sinews to set in. He stumbled in mid-air and went fluttering to the ground. He pecked at some seeds lying among the leaves and needles and became aware all at once of an overpowering thirst. He raised his head, seeking the scent of water.

Dickens hopped along the ground, fluttering his wings a bit to test the quality of the pain and to reassure himself that he was not yet helpless. He went to a stump of a tree fallen so long ago that it was hollowed out with rot. The water of the last rain lay in the chalice of it, not clear but palatable. He drank and felt the better for it.

There was a shallow ledge within the hollow stump. An inch or two of water covered it. Dickens hopped into it and refreshed himself, spreading his wings and sending a flurry of spray into the air where it irised in a late beam of sunlight.

A long, slender shape slipped through the undergrowth, treading softly on the carpet of needles upon the earth, the weasel, the deprived hunter given another chance for prey.

Dickens hopped up on the rim of the tree stump, saw the shadow of the weasel as it approached and, charged with new fear, leaped into the air, beating his wings, beyond the pain. He flew to the heights of a pine tree and took refuge there, his heart beating wildly. He cocked his head and saw the weasel circling far below, raising its head from time to time, mouth agape, little teeth sharp as blades and white as stone.

Dickens nodded, exhausted again. Such weariness as he'd never felt before. Not even when he was young and new to the training.

The young birds had been brought along to flights to loft of twenty-five miles along the northeast flight path usually flown by the Rochester Pigeon Union Club. Now Da meant to increase the distance and test the birds that had shown their mettle against a range doubled in one fell swoop. A test of heart and stamina.

We drove out early on a late summer morning. There was already a hint of September in the air, promising vigor. We were mostly quiet together, in the comfortable way of old companions. From time to time one or the other of us made some comment on the passing countryside.

We were more than seventy-three miles beyond the outskirts of Rochester, but only fifty as the pigeons would fly, on the northern edge of the Tonawanda Indian Reservation. Da parked the pickup on the rim of a posted meadow. We released the birds and watched them until they were dancing dots against the blue. We leaned against the truck, meaning to tarry awhile.

"Look there," Da said, pointing to the meadow beyond the wire strands of the fence. "Do you see?"

"What?" I asked.

"The tracks."

"Those wagon tracks through the meadow?" I said, disappointed, having expected wonders.

"Yes, those."

I relaxed again and Da smiled.

"Doesn't seem like much, does it?"

"Just wagon tracks," I said.

"What do you reckon made them?"

"Farm cart, I suppose."

"I don't think so. I think they were tracks made more than a hundred years ago by a covered wagon. Some pioneer family took this way going on to Fort Wayne to join up with some train traveling west."

I perked up a bit at that.

"Would wagon marks last so long?" I wondered.

"They do. A meadow is a delicate and tender thing. If you were to put your foot on it, months might go by before the scar was completely gone away."

That was something to think about.

Even as we talked of those olden times and the hard imprint that people made upon the land, the changes wrought in a lifetime and less, clouds were massing up above the hills in the direction toward which the pigeons flew. Da first became aware of them.

"That's not so good," he said, straightening up and squinting his eyes. "Let's get back home."

We got into the cab of the truck and started off along the dirt road toward the highway. By the time we reached it the first rain was falling and it was clear that the storm we were driving into was in full force over the land ahead. In half an hour the rain was falling in torrents, sluicing along the roadway, making the ditches at the sides run reddish with muddy water.

When we reached home, none of the birds in training had arrived. Da went to the mud porch and brought out slickers and rubber boots for us and we went down to the lofts to wait.

Our kit of racing birds had flown dead on into the storm. They were blown about and separated. The landmarks they sought out were altered and obscured by rain driven by the wind. They'd been slowed down, scattered farther, flying closer to the ground, straining their eyes for familiar features. Their plumage had become soaked and sodden.

Dickens made it home to the loft first.

He'd trapped without hesitation, eager to seek the shelter of the loft, the warmth of his nest box. He was trembling with the wet, chilled to the bone, terrified by the experience of the storm. But he'd flown as straight to home as he was able.

Some of the birds were lost and never found again. The rest straggled in over a period of hours.

I held Dickens in my hands, warming him, feeding him choice bits of grain. Da looked at the bird with a kind of excitement, that feeling a sportsman gets when he's bred a superior creature, be it dog or horse or pigeon.

"What is it, Da?" I asked.

He grinned from ear to ear, laughed high in his throat, scarcely able to contain his feelings and his pleasure.

"I think we've bred us a champion to beat all champions," he said. "Your Dickens will surely end up in the pigeon hall of fame. Sometimes it happens. You work and strive for years and that one creature comes along. At first you're not quite sure. A thousand birds have passed under your hands and eyes. Then one day it happens. Something that proves the worth of the creature. You look and you wonder why you'd never seen it from the very start. You've bred a proper wonder."

I'd never heard Da go on over any pigeon we'd ever raised or flown. It startled me. I looked at Dickens nestled in my hands with eyes that had never quite seen him before; I seemed to see new excellence in him just as Da said. Dickens *was* a champion. Or, at least, he'd soon have his chance to prove it.

But first Da intended to further test Dickens's homing determination. Day after day we took Dickens out alone—not neglecting altogether the training of the other birds—and flew him from several points of the compass.

Each time, with surprisingly little confusion or hesitation my wonderful bird took his bearings and flew straight to the loft. Da was most impressed.

"Now look there," he'd said the tenth time or so that Dickens had struck out unerringly in the direction of the loft. "There's a theory that a pigeon flies home by instinct alone."

"What *is* instinct, Da?"

He thought a moment and said, "Instinct is a natural faculty like sight or smell or taste, not really evident. Some sort of adaptation valuable to the creature that has it, natural as breathing and as little thought about. Now if anyone was to look at Dickens making straight for home, they would suppose, maybe, that all pigeons did the same."

"They don't," I said. "Most just circle around wider and wider, before they strike out."

"And some never make it home at all," Da agreed. "Now, some say it's the sun that guides the homeward flight. Seems sensible. We lost enough birds in that storm when there was no sun to see. Some hold with the idea that some magnetic lines of force lead them home just like a road takes us where we want to go."

"What do you think it is?" I asked.

"Two things mostly. A sharp eye and a clever memory. Things that birds have, more or less, just like people. When Dickens flies out of a new direction, from strange territory, he reaches higher before making for home. Did you notice that?"

"Yes," I said.

"Getting a perspective on things, I'd say. Climbing high to catch some distant mark on the land that gives him a clue of where he is. Your Dickens has a little brain filled with more shapes of trees and folds in the land than we could ever imagine. We've helped his talents grow. But it's in him to be great. He's got eye and brain. Most of all he has heart and grit. That makes a winner."

On the way home I was silent. Da finally remarked on how quiet I was.

"What are you thinking about, Hugh?" he asked.

"How Dickens gets up high to see as much as he can before he goes one way or another."

"What about it?" Da said.

"Just seems to me that it's a smart thing for anybody to do when they're not sure what they're on about."

"Well," my grandfather said, smiling in a proud way. "Well, well, well."

I petted Dickens much that day. A stout-hearted bird lies quietly in the hand. Dickens cooed, remained nearly motionless except for alert glances thrown here and there. Quite content.

What is the limit of pigeon recall?

Dickens nodded among his memories. Times as distant yet as luminous as the moon that sailed the sky, shedding its light on the forest, building shadows.

A rabbit left a patch of darkness on the ground. A great horned owl left the limb of the tree below Dickens's perch. It was dark brown, mottled in white tinged with buff, its wings darker shrouds. It wore a locket of white at its throat and its beak was black as death. Its great eyes shone deep yellow. The talons were black as well. It slipped through the air soundlessly. Downy filaments at the bases of the feathers cushioned the passage of air through its wings. There was a scream in the dark. A flash of scarlet in the moonlight. Dickens watched as the nocturnal hunter carried its prey to a private feeding place. The weasel had been taken.

A raccoon left its den in the bole of a hollow tree and went off scavenging, a thief, masked and stealthy.

A barn owl slipped through the forest, struck at a wood rat, missed and, with a look of perfect calm upon its otherworldly face, flew off, patient and confident.

The life of the night wood went on as Dickens rested, safe but discontent.

There has been of late all sorts of discussion, articles written, panels assembled, results announced, concerning the inability of one generation to communicate with the next. Perhaps it would be better said that there's been a new rush of it, for the subject has been explored, I'm sure, as long as men have mused upon such things, frustrated because an intimacy they feel should be evident and unforced is, instead, a kind of combat. I'm told this by my friends, hurt and much confused.

I enjoy a relationship with the young that seems a wonder to those same friends. It should be quite clear to them that I pose no threat to their sons. To ask my advice is no dishonor to my young friends. I'm not expected to use the relationship of teacher to pupil against them at some later date. I'm detached from rivalry.

I know how fortunate I've been in having Da as my playmate and companion, my teacher and confidant. It did, I know, make my relationship to my father comfortable and loving. I didn't seek a pal in him but a father who would stand between me and any real terrors.

Da and I, on the other hand, were conspirators together, flying pleasure as our banner. Does anyone ever comment on the fact of the hard work the young—and the old—put into play?

I think now of all those dark mornings, the cold of four o'clock Septembers and Octobers when he and I would trod the fields crisp with rime, ice ponds formed along the edges of the stream until the stream itself froze in mid-motion, or so it seemed.

Even now the special smell of autumn rises to my nostrils at the memory, burning them, pinching them with fingers of delight. Crisp blades of grass crunch under my feet and I feel my grandfather's hand resting on my shoulder.

# *Ten*

My Da lay helpless, attended to, moved about from side to side, cooed and chuckled at by this nurse and that, probed and poked at by a clutch of doctors as busy in their chesty importance as any kit of pouter pigeons.

I went with my mother to visit in the morning just before school. He was asleep, seemed to be, pretended to be perhaps. I went again at the noon hour and he was still lying there with his eyes closed, his mouth empty and twisted to the side. It frightened me terribly.

I was found by the nurse called Miss Pryor and shooed gently from the room. Dr. Sand was walking down the corridor. He was a kindly man, I suppose, though he seemed aloof and forbidding to me since I believed that my grandfather's fate was, somehow, in his hands. I looked at them. They were very smooth, the nails carefully trimmed and flawlessly clean. I expected that was a good sign, but I'd come to think that capable hands were those that were a bit grimy with use, a bit scarred, nicked, and abraded; worn by work and years. My grandfather's hands.

"What are you doing here, Hugh?"

"Come to see my Da."

"Who brought you? Is your mother here?"

I shook my head, suddenly afraid that I would be forbidden the company of my grandfather hereafter because I'd broken some rule of which I'd been unaware.

"Your father?"

I shook my head.

"You walked all the way from school?"

I nodded hesitantly. He saw that I was afraid and put his hand on my shoulder. It's a gesture grown-ups have to comfort and soothe the young.

"I'll drive you back," he said.

As we drove he chattered about my school, the end of lessons in a week or so, and the vacation that stretched before me. I was suddenly overwhelmed by the prospect of a summer without my grandfather to help me live it. I felt a panic that made my limbs grow rigid. For the first time in my life, I faced the idea of irreparable loss. I must have made some sound, for he put his hand on my knee.

"Is my grandfather going to die?" I asked in a rush.

Dr. Sand hesitated, wanting to comfort but not wanting to lie and destroy a child's faith in truth.

"He's an old man," he said. That wasn't enough and he knew it. "We can't be certain,

Hugh. He's strong, but he's old. This—accident —will leave him diminished even if he makes a strong recovery. You understand that?"

"Yes."

But will he die? I wanted to shout. I didn't care if my Da and I couldn't walk the fields together, fly the pigeons from our hands, wait through the miracle of hatching eggs. I wanted my grandfather even if he were motionless but for his eyes. Even if he—

My thoughts stopped all at once as though thrust against a barrier. I saw how selfish I'd become. I was willing to have a strong old man lie trapped in a useless body because of my refusal to give him up to some final comfort. I saw death differently in the moment.

"We have hope," Dr. Sand said.

And I nodded my head, meaning that my hopes were that my grandfather should pass on with all the dignity that he desired. I would help him in that in any way that I was able. I felt a certain calm fall over me like a cloak.

Dickens had been aloft since first light. The night predators were gone to nest and den, the peregrine was not in the sky. He'd tested his wings and cried out in pain, but the discomfort was bearable and he'd risen into the air from the shadowed wood and set his path for home again.

Far away frigid winds had swept down the broad reaches of Quebec, smashed into the juvenile storm spawned over Lake Winnepeg and drove it southwest across Green Bay and La Crosse. Then the northern mass lost some of its thrust. Its energy became caught up in the storm's eddy. Direction was changed again and the storm grew in ferocity as it picked up speed and smashed southeast. Rain fell across eastern Michigan and northern Ohio. It was cold and hard.

Dickens flew into it over Lima when the wind had changed direction once more and was blowing powerfully at half-gale strength toward the south.

He fought against it but, even had he lost none of his power in the encounter with the peregrine, he'd never have been able to withstand the fury of the winds. He didn't give up. Neither was he afraid.

My own fears were in control.

I left school at noon and didn't return. I don't think anyone would have said anything to me even if it weren't the last week and nothing much going on except class parties and summer good-byes to schoolmates, some of whom would not be seen again till autumn.

I hung around the lofts, cleaning the porches and pens, changing the water and flying the birds. I scanned the sky quite often, hoping for a sight of Dickens, Moonbeam, or Jenny, not so much because I believed they'd have flown so far so fast but because I wanted some news to take to my grandfather when my parents and I went to visit him that evening. There was no sign of them.

I called up the pigeon club and was told a storm had cut across the flight path. Most all the birds had been past the edges of it in time, but some might have been caught up in the trailing edge of it as it spiraled across the land.

"Stragglers, maybe," I said to the secretary, "but that wouldn't be Dickens, even if Jenny and Moonbeam had been caught in the smash."

"How's your grandfather?" the secretary, Mr. Englund, asked.

"Better," I said, not really knowing if that was true or not but expecting it's what my Da would want to say so as not to make him seem pitiable.

"We'll be to see him this evening. Will that be all right?"

I hesitated. Some instinct told me my grandfather would rather not have a bunch of people, even friends, hovering about and clucking their tongues over him or, worse, making all sorts of two-faced remarks about how well he looked. Simple politeness had to be considered, however; Da put much stock in that.

"Well, we'll call up and ask at the reception. Just a few might come. Not a whole mob of us, Hugh."

"That would be fine."

"Shall I call you if the birds start homing?" Mr. Englund asked. "Will you be at Henri's house?"

I said that I would and found, even as restless as I felt, that I'd trapped myself into staying inside by the phone. At three twenty-six Mr. Englund did call. Mr Fouquet's racer, Windhill, had trapped in good time. The winner couldn't be known until all the leaders were in and their time computed into the air-line distances, but one thing was sure—no bird of ours would win since none was home and our loft was closest to Hillsboro.

Tears came up in my eyes. I scolded myself for even caring about such things when my grandfather was threatened the way he was.

Moonbeam came home an hour later and Jenny just a few minutes after that, but Dickens was nowhere in sight. I cried then because I feared I'd lost the bird and was afraid that was a terrible sign that I would lose my grandfather as well.

I had that bad news to give to my grandfather when we went to visit him that evening. He was awake, freshly bathed. His hair was combed. He looked less fragile against the pillows that propped him up. His eyes were on the door as we walked in and he smiled, showing his teeth. The smile was distorted but I realized, with a start, that I was already becoming used to it and found comfort in the greater strength I believed I now saw in it.

He surprised us further by lifting up his right arm almost to the level of his shoulder. Miss Pryor stood by, beaming at his accomplishment as though she'd taught a babe to walk. Da glanced at her in a wicked way as she made little approving sounds with her lips. My father smiled, greatly relieved at this sign of improvement, taking a great breath as though sharing the effort. I wondered in the moment what he must be feeling. How different might the quality of his love for Da be than mine? He was more intimately flesh of Da's flesh. Were his father's pains more surely felt in his own body?

He'd brought an electric razor. My grandfather's beard had grown in the three days since he'd been stricken. My father plugged it in and began to shave my grandfather, who tried to raise his chin a bit to make it easier and looked at my father from the corner of his eyes with deep affection. It was almost as though he were making a gift of his helplessness.

I don't believe I've ever since seen an activity so full of love. It startled and shook me. I was seeing life and something of its meaning in nearly every act and motion, acutely, through the lens of my own emotion.

It touched my father, I know, because he hurried at the end, unplugged the razor, and made the poor excuse that he wanted to put it back in the glove compartment of the car for fear he'd forget it and fail to have it for himself in the morning, just so that he might leave the room.

My mother left as well to have some conference with Miss Pryor about my grandfather's comfort, and Da and I were left alone.

He patted the bed and I went to sit on it. He took my hand and I nearly cried out at the power with which he gripped it. It pleased me.

He let my hand go, and I reached in my pocket
for the gift I'd brought to him to tell him that
he and I mustn't be impatient with the waiting
that might face us both.

It always amazes me when I count the many
ways in which a moment can be vividly recalled;
so vividly that it is somehow more real in the
memory than it was in the living. Questions arise
about whether or not we live so much as *relive*
life. Do we know where we've been only after
we've returned? Do we feel the pressure of lips
and hands, soft and plump, only after they've
grown dry and thin with age? All this is idle.
What really matters is the fact that the sound
of a distant bell can awaken in the heart the
moment when one walked along the path to the
church on one's wedding day; the faintest flavor
of mint recalls iced tea and a hundred marvelous
picnics, the sight of a curl of blue smoke beyond
a hill brings back the memory of a single rare
day that is all autumn days, and the touch of a
small homemade lucky piece makes one a child
again.

# Eleven

My gift was a peach pit Da had carved into the strangely amusing shape of two monkeys sitting face to face. Kissing, if monkeys kiss. Da insisted that they did. It had been given me as a kind of trophy for a race that was lost. The first one Dickens ever flew.

Before setting my bird out against that first challenge, we'd mated him. I was so familiar with the process that one would imagine it should seem commonplace to me, but I never lost my wonder at the visible demonstration of falling in love evidenced by the birds. Perhaps that was because Da, who was so much older than I, had quite clearly never lost his wonder of it and made my senses more attuned to the marvel.

Dickens, like other pigeons, had left the nest when he was about five weeks old, not because he wanted to but because hunger tricked him. Angel had come to feed his offspring less and less. Spotting him near the nest and eager for a meal, both Dickens and Scrooge tried to reach him, tumbled from the nest for the first time, flapped their wings, and did, in a manner of speaking, complete their first flight.

For a few nights they continued to roost in their old nest box with the adults, but as soon as they'd learned to forage for themselves we removed them both and placed them with other young bachelors in a separate loft.

Cock pigeons are an aggressive bunch, bold and always ready to accept a challenge over territorial rights. They walk about like schoolboys with chips on their shoulders daring other birds to knock them off. Dickens was bigger, brasher, more aggressive than any of his mates and had become, perhaps, a bit of a bully. Only his nest mate, Scrooge, never tired of presenting himself for a quarrel. Then there'd be much wing-flapping, pecking, and significant cooing until Scrooge did, at last, back off.

The hens are made of gentler stuff as seems usual among the majority of God's creations, though they are often fiercer in their defense of the young. We had one pigeon, fragile, nearly white, with a pearly eye, delicate as a china cup who, wounded and bleeding, yet fought off the attack of a raiding possum which had come to take her chicks. It was she, Thalia, named for the muse of pastoral poetry, meaning "the blooming one"—my grandfather told me—who had lost her mate through mischance and which we chose to become Dickens's wife if she'd have him. She was older than Dickens by two years.

"And wiser," Da said. "Dickens is too big for his breeches, lording it over his loft mates the way he does."

I didn't know whether I should feel shame or pride that my bird was the unchallenged master of his territory. Pride, I think, won out, and Da knew it. So perhaps Dickens's lesson was mine as well.

We introduced them to one another and stepped away for the sake of their privacy. Dickens walked around Thalia several times and began his mating dance. He spread his wings and dragged his tail to show his form to best advantage. The widow cocked an eye at him, measuring him, determining his ardor, listening to his murmured promises. She was not a young maiden easily seduced by any passing suitor, but a matron of some maturity who clearly meant to take and keep the upper hand. It was some time before she surrendered, but when she did, it was done in so expert and sweetly aggressive a manner that we laughed, Da and I, as Dickens scrambled away in confusion.

When their marriage was consummated, Dickens hurried off to find them a home as Thalia walked delicately around the porch sunning herself and softly blinking her eyes.

He bustled about, eyeing this half-shadowed nest box or that unoccupied one washed by the sun. He made the choice of one discreetly located, entered it, announced his possession, then called out loudly to his wife that she should come and approve his selection. He crouched in the new home, shaking his wing tips as he awaited her arrival. She came with some display of eagerness, looked over the dwelling, and walked away. It's a rare thing for a female not to accept the nest site chosen by the male. But Thalia had a nest box of her own and apparently she wanted no change of domicile. Gently, ever careful of his pride and dignity, she led him to her home and offered it to him.

Dickens resisted for a while but finally, in a flurry of activity, he threw out the material of her nest and went out to seek fresh sticks and straw and leaves. Thalia selected what she wanted of the pile that he gathered, turning and twisting slowly, piling it around her body until the nest was built.

She laid her clutch of eggs ten days after the mating, driven to the nest by frequent peckings delivered by Dickens whose instincts told him that it was time for the laying. They sat the eggs and, in proper time, the young squabs were born. When they were eight days old, we took Dickens from the nest box and placed him in the basket.

He was entered in a race of three hundred miles, his first. Da might have held him for longer races right from the beginning, but I think he realized how eager I was to have Dickens tested against the clock and other racers. I can't be sure if that was the reason for Dickens's loss. There are a few rare birds that fly as well at all distances, but apparently Dickens was for the long race alone. The three-hundred-miler ended in disappointment for me. Dickens arrived well behind the leaders, at a speed which wouldn't have been agreeable even in a far less promising bird.

I was foolish about it, pouting and a little angry with my pet.

Da came down from the lofts to where I sat by the stream looking at the icy waters carrying autumn leaves away.

He sat down quietly beside me, never suggesting that I might be cold sitting on the ground that way, allowing me for the moment to be as heavy with my disappointment as I wished to be. He held a jackknife in one hand and a dried peach pit in the other. The blade made a thin scraping noise on the nut. A smell rose from it that was delicious and somehow mysterious. I finally looked to see what he was about.

"Dickens didn't do well," Da said.

"No," I replied, hearing the harshness in my own voice.

"Had high hopes for winning, didn't you?"

"Yes," I said less harshly.

"He let you down."

"Yes," I said.

Da was quiet for a while, giving his attention to the little carving in his hand.

"Did he have a right to let you down?" he asked all at once.

"What do you mean?" I asked, startled at the question, not really understanding it.

"Did he do it deliberately?"

"Never," I said.

"Did he do his best, do you think?"

"Yes," I said after a time.

"Have we done our best for him?"

"We could always do better," I said, for that was the thing Da always said about nearly any job that didn't come off exactly right.

"How?"

"I don't know."

"What don't you know?"

"What went wrong. Why Dickens lost."

"We'll send him out in training over and over again until we find out why he didn't come straight to home. Even then," Da said, "we may never know. You've got to accept the fact that life is filled with little mysteries."

I was watching when he cut his eyes at me to see if I was attending the lesson. He laughed when I caught him at it and I laughed too.

"And disappointments too," I said.

"Indeed."

He examined the carving in his hand and found it good, for he closed the knife and put it in his pocket. He rubbed the fruit stone on his sweater.

"So what's the only thing you've really lost so far, since you've still got Dickens in the loft ready to try again?"

"Just a trophy," I said.

He grinned and pressed the peach pit into my hand.

"And now you've got one of those. This is for you and Dickens. Win or lose, he finished the race."

So, many months later, I took that little trophy of a race that was worthy because completed and put it back into my grandfather's hand from where it had come.

He glanced at it and tried to smile.

"Hey, Da," I said and could say no more for a while.

I have that little curiosity with me now. It was a precious part of the estate that was left to me. It's grown very smooth and highly polished with the touch of my hands over the years; the carving has been smoothed away so that only someone who knew the secret of its design could see two loving monkeys there.

Holding it to my lips I can still smell the faint odor of peach, or imagine that I do. A summer smell. And that, in turn, recalls a day in summer when Da and I decided to dam up a portion of the stream below the house and make a swimming hole, or at least a wading pond, of a portion of it. Even the most fanatic fanciers couldn't occupy themselves with pigeons every spare hour of the day. Especially those long hours of June, July, and August.

We searched along the banks of the stream among the trees for rocks of sufficient size to make a base for our dam. Together we spent two hours digging out a boulder that seemed wedded to the center of the earth and rolling it to the side of the rushing stream. We looked at one another, eyes sparkling, holding laughter in our mouths and bellies in anticipation of the wonderful splash that was coming. Then we pushed that huge boulder all together, to see it slip down the bank side, gouging out its own path, balanced, refusing to roll over in a glorious rush. It settled like some dignified old dowager sitting into an easy chair, entering the water with scarely a ripple. How we laughed at that.

There were other rocks that responded better for us. We were wet nearly through long before there was anything that looked like a dam. Now we had only to wait until the stream filled up the basin behind it and overflowed the banks at that spot where they were lowest. A couple of hours should provide us with swimming depth. We went back inside to have a bite and wait.

A summer storm arose, swift and without warning. The skies were black all at once and opened up a flood of rain. The stream grew even as we watched it from the shelter of the mud porch. A glut of last year's leaves, the limbs of trees, even a small log or two came tumbling down the torrent. The cloudburst tore apart our dam and, foolishly, we cheered because there was something glorious in the sight.

We never did try to make another swimming hole. I can see now that our engineering was faulty. No such accommodation could have been created in the middle of the stream the way Da and I had gone about it. What we'd had was another day together.

I wish I could have such a day again, some

hours of foolish labor. I wish I could care enough to excavate some huge boulder and send it crashing, or even sliding gently, into some woodland stream.

# Twelve

I found my voice before my mother and father returned. I'd placed the peach pit in his hand and Da had looked at me in such a way that I knew he understood my meaning.

"Mr. Fouquet's Windhill came to the loft at three twenty-six," I said. "Moonbeam and Jenny have come home. And all the other birds but seven. Dickens never came home. There was a storm out over Ohio. I reckon he's been lost in it."

Da made a slight movement as though shaking his head. He frowned a bit.

Dickens had been captured by the storm but was not yet altogether lost. A full-blown gale had blown him farther and farther south. He'd been buffeted about like an autumn leaf, expending prodigious amounts of energy just to stay aloft, pushed off to the rim of the storm, whirled about over the valley of the Cumberland River in Kentucky and on across the border into Tennessee.

He managed to break loose and, exhausted, fluttered wet and torn, to the shelter to the marshlands around Falling Water, more than three hundred and fifty miles off course and seven hundred on a straight air-line to home.

He huddled among the reeds listening to the strange sounds of the water birds protesting the weather. Two or three ducks quarreled among themselves and swam in placid circles.

Da looked at me with some question in his eyes and murmured something I tried to understand and thought I did.

"No, Da, I don't think Dickens failed me. I know that he didn't. Still he's lost."

My grandfather spoke again, a harsh sound not only because the words were still unintelligible but because there was a determination in his voice to make me hold on to hope.

"We won't give up on Dickens," I thought he said.

"But if the storm's thrown him far away, how can we expect him to see his way to home? You said pigeons came home because of a sharp eye and a clever memory."

He gripped my hand to stop my words.

He grinned. "I—would—would—no—*could* . . . I could wrong. Could be wrong."

The words came out all in a sentence. He breathed hard as though he'd run a long race but grinned fit to bust. He'd heard himself speak sensibly. But when he tried again it came out all gibberish and I told him not to try anymore.

Mr. Fouquet arrived then, poking his head around the hospital door like a turtle peering from his shell.

"You old fool," he said to my grandfather.

He nodded to me and drew up a chair beside the bed. He put a gift-wrapped box on the side table.

"Candy," he said.

Da waved his right hand.

"No, thanks," Fouquet said. "Bad for the teeth." He smiled, showing his own, most of them intact. One of the ways in which he claimed small victories over his old friend.

"The times have been calculated," he went on. "Windhill's the winner at eight hundred sixteen point sixty-five yards per minute. I'm sorry about Dickens."

He looked at me.

"Don't give up hope."

I said that I wouldn't. Then I noticed that he'd reached over and taken my grandfather's hand for a moment, given it a squeeze. The message was as much for Da as for me. Da must have squeezed back, for Fouquet smiled, pleased at Da's will to fight.

It recalled a day to me when I'd come home from school with a bloody nose and bruises alongside my jaw. I mean to say I went to Da's house because I could expect my mother to make something of a fuss over the damage done to me and the fact that I'd risen to the challenge of a fist-fight against her constant warnings.

Da was neutral as he bathed my face with cold water.

"What started it?" he asked.

I shrugged my shoulders.

"Don't want to say?"

"Can't remember," I said.

"Something pretty small then."

"I guess."

"Don't know?"

"Don't know."

"Foolish, wasn't it?"

"I couldn't back down," I said. "You wouldn't have wanted me to run away, would you?"

"Why not?"

"It'd be cowardly," I said in a soldierly way.

"Ah. So you took to punching at this other fellow and he at you because your friends would think you afraid if you didn't?"

I nodded hesitantly, feeling a little lesson on its way and just annoyed enough not to want to hear it. I wasn't always eager to drink in my grandfather's wisdom.

"Couldn't talk it out?" he went on.

"Didn't try."

"Ah."

"I know I acted foolish," I said before he could say it for me.

"Not necessarily," he said, surprising me. "Probably, but not necessarily."

"Is that all?" I finally asked when he didn't say any more.

He grinned. "Waiting for some advice from Grandpa's Almanac?" he teased.

He'd put me in the temper to hear what he had to say.

"All right, then, here it is. Never fight over anything small."

My heart sank a bit. In his mild way it sounded like he was scolding me.

"Unless," he added, "you're ready to go to the wall for it."

"The wall?"

"To the end of your strength."

"I kept swinging until I couldn't lift my arms," I said, wanting to make him proud of me about that at least.

"In the name of your honor?"

"Yes."

"And did you exercise compassion?"

Well, Roger hadn't hollered "Quits!" so I hadn't the chance to display any real forbearance. On the other hand, nobody won the fight, so I guess we showed compassion enough.

"How can you know if something's small? Who can you ask?" I wanted to know.

He shook his head. "That's for you and you alone to say."

Now Da was in a fight, but it certainly wasn't for anything small. It was for his life and, perhaps even more importantly, for his dignity.

Fouquet and Da bantered back and forth.

Strange way to put it since Da's friend did all the talking and Da merely murmured now and then.

Finally Da's old friend left. I thought the visit long but I suppose it was really very short, just a token to let my grandfather know that all the men and women he knew in the pigeon club were concerned about him. That pleased Da, I know. He held great store by the respect people gave to him because, by his way of thinking, it was the best of what a man earned with his life.

My mother and father took me home right after Mr. Fouquet left. Da was growing visibly tired. He tried to smile as Mother kissed him on the corner of his mouth. He gripped my hand and looked into my father's eyes as though making certain he wouldn't forget the lines of his son's face before morning. Or was there some other question there? Was he asking how they intended disposing of his sick old body? He had no power over his destiny anymore and had to look to his son to sustain him in this trial.

I didn't sleep well, imagining that Da was back at his own house standing by the loft waiting, without me, for Dickens to come home.

I heard my mother's light voice from time to time through the night answering my father who spoke in long stretches about how to handle the new responsibilities created by Da's illness. His voice was deep and rumbled like a distant storm.

Thinking back on it now, I know that the worst part of it all for Da must have been that dependency he had thrust upon him. I mean to say, he'd had a son and watched him grow, shared the years with him and felt that his was the guiding hand as much as such things are possible, and then, all of a sudden, like a bolt of lightning, a thunderclap, his wasn't the power. He'd been supplanted as the head of the family by a man he could not help but remember as a boy coming to him with some hurt or with some triumph. He was suddenly the helpless creature, the child, and that boy was now the man, making decisions that bore sharply upon his life. In that way the flesh of his flesh had become the enemy, just as I clearly see that the father is, in some ways, the enemy of the boy, thwarting him and shrinking the borders of his dreams and aspirations.

In gripping my hand my grandfather had made a pact with me across the years, saying to me that we were both weak and must depend on one another to protect one another against the kind, benevolent judgments of those who would be our caretakers.

# Thirteen

When the dawn came up again, Dickens roused himself. Ducks were making a racket all around him, quarreling among themselves.

Among the reeds Claude Shipley and his son, Ray, were hunkered into a blind fashioned with skillful hands around their rowboat. They were good companions, taking their recreation and sport together since Ray'd been six or seven. Now he was ten and could fish and hunt with the patience of a man, settling himself beside a stream unmoving with rod and reel or squatting in a marsh waiting for ducks to rise on a wet morning.

Ray had his own shotgun, a light over-and-under, that he was able to use with better than average marksmanship. It rested across his knees. He glanced over at his father and smiled as they both felt their nerve ends tingling at the sound of the marshland coming to life.

Dickens was perched out on the limb of a willow burnt leafless in some old fire. He tried his wings and found the muscles of his breast and shoulder better than they'd been when freshly torn. Some good healing had taken place. The battering of the storm had taken its toll in energy, not in pain.

He cocked his head and looked up toward the sky. It was clear as a crystal pond, not a trace of cloud, swept clean by the storm, and that invigorated him, bringing back sharp memories of the brook that ran down to the Genesee. Little dots appeared a long way off in the blue. Tiny voices called in the morning air.

The few ducks that were using the marsh called out to their brethren. Dickens watched as the ducks came drifting down out of the sky. He was homesick and wanted the company of his own kind when he saw these birds all flocked together. He rose into the sky.

Ray and Claude saw the birds coming down out of the blue, quacking away. They scarcely noticed the pigeon flying up as though to meet the ducks. Claude tapped his son's shoulder, giving him the first shot.

Ray lifted the shotgun to his shoulder at the ducks as they came into range, just as Dickens spiraled to pass the edge of the flock, reaching for altitude in hopes that he could find his way to home. Ray fired one barrel. Scattered bits of fire flashed through Dickens's wing. He tottered in mid-air and saw with horror that one of the mallards was gone limp, falling like a stone to splash into the reflecting water below.

There was a wetness along his side. He left a fragile bloody wake behind him as he flew off in desperate effort to get beyond the range of death.

He flew despite the old injuries and the new wounds. He flew although there was nothing that presented itself to his eye or memory that gave him any clue that he was flying in the right direction.

Perhaps in that Da had been wrong, for Dickens flew toward the northeast, not on a beeline for Rochester it's true, but northeast all the same, led along by some tiny bell of instinct that rang in his head and heart. He progressed slowly but steadily along the path over Tennessee and Kentucky. When night began to fall he was almost at the border of Ohio, still very, very far from home.

Da was far from better. The little improvement that appeared so promising, when he'd managed to lift his arm and later speak that one intelligible sentence, seemed to fade away. The luster in his eye when he'd spoken, or listened, to Fouquet seemed to dim and he lay on his side staring out the window. I found him just so each time I went to see him to tell him that Dickens wasn't home. As Da's strength failed, my hopes that Dickens would come back, bolstered by my grandfather's spirit in me, began to weaken as well. Most of what I believed was linked to my grandfather's wisdom, hope, and strength, one way or another.

That night when Dickens was roosting nearly four hundred miles from home, my grandfather stared out into the dark, thinking thoughts I couldn't imagine, waiting for something I couldn't conceive.

I knew of death. It was no surprise to me, though in human terms it was largely a stranger. Animals had died in my view and birds in my hands, but the death of someone close had been an experience observed only from a distance. The very nearest I'd ever been was when Mr. Watkins, the oldest member of the Rochester Pigeon Club, passed away in his ninety-seventh year. He'd been friendly to me in the vague way of the very old, patting me on the hand or head and staring into my face as though it were full of secrets he wished to know. His eyes, at first, had frightened me, for they were pale as a workshirt that had suffered too many washings, threatening to come all apart if touched or even looked at too hard. But soon enough I saw his eyes to be much as he was, simply gentle and fragile, short-sighted because there was no need any longer to see too far.

I dressed in my Sunday suit to go to his funeral. Da had left that choice up to me, after first explaining that no one would think less of me if I didn't go to pay my respects to an ancient who was more acquaintance than friend but that Mr. Watkins's relatives would be pleased by such a gesture if I did go. It would lead them to feel that their old patriarch had lived his life, even making new young friends, right till the end.

I'd have gone in any case because I must admit to having had a certain natural curiosity and invited the opportunity to see a dead person up close.

There was nothing special to it. I suppose I was a touch afraid, for such stillness even in someone only asleep is, somehow, more than a little terrifying. I knelt on the prayer stool beside the coffin and bent my head over my folded hands in a prayer, the shortest that I knew. I looked up sharply at Mr. Watkins because I had the sudden feeling that he was watching me, but, of course, his eyes were closed, thinly waxen. I could see there was lip rouge on his mouth and that, perhaps, was the most disturbing thing about it as far as I was concerned. I felt that Mr. Watkins had been made a fool of and said so to my grandfather on the way home.

He laughed softly, as though pleased by something good I'd done. I later knew it was because he reckoned he had quite evidently helped to make me clear-eyed and impatient with fraud.

"Little attendances upon the dead, Hugh. Just some little touch to ease the harshness. Foolish in its way. You saw that."

"He should have had his own face to carry away with him," I said haltingly, trying, myself, to know what I meant even as I said it.

Da squeezed my shoulder.

"You'll see that I have my own face, won't you, Hugh?"

I started as though he'd struck me. He clamped his hand on my shoulder as we walked.

"My own face, my own suit on my back—not a new one bought for the occasion—and make sure they put shoes on my feet even if they can't be seen." He took his hand from my shoulder then and roughed my hair. "Listen to me putting burdens on a boy," he said.

"I'll see to it, Da—" I said.

"One more thing—" he said. "I was born in a bed at home. I saw my children born the same way. I want to die likewise. Strange cradles don't make comfortable biers."

So that was about all I knew of death until that time. I felt it outside among the trees and shadows as Da lay in bed and Dickens remained lost to me. In fact, I was certain by then that Dickens had met death and been touched by him after he told the shadow the way to my grandfather.

I couldn't know that he was still alive among the streets and alleys of the town where he was forced to roost with the coming of night.

Much of what the old teach the young seems to have a lot to do with responsibility, honor, and trust. The promise I so willingly gave to Da, though never thinking it would ever really be asked of me since Da would surely live forever, was not the only responsibility he'd ever placed upon me. There was the matter of the key to the small room in which we kept the wicker baskets, the feed and other gear concerned with the raising and racing of pigeons. It was kept locked not so much from fear of theft but inadvertent contamination of the seed grains we fed our pets. Da was always prudent and knew people were often thoughtless or careless.

Business was taking him away from home for a week or so, some convention of typesetters. He'd been asked to address them about the early days. The pigeons would be entirely in my care and I suppose Da wondered if it were too much responsibility to give to a nine-year-old.

He asked me into the parlor and said, "I have a little piece of advice for you, Hugh."

"What?" I asked, knowing he wanted me to attend him closely by the simple gravity of his manner.

"Never let anyone give you a key you don't want."

I suppose I frowned, not knowing what he meant.

"You can tell the amount of a man's concerns by the number of keys he carries," Da said. "Never take one unles you mean to accept the responsibility that goes with it."

I understood then and nodded my head.

He handed me the key to the storeroom. It gleamed in the last light coming through the parlor window. I didn't touch it at first. I knew it wasn't simply the key to a lock that protected a few sacks of feed and several woven baskets but a symbol of a share of manhood he was offering to me. There was an air of uncommon drama about the act.

I took the key.

It was later that I took the "key" of the ceremony surrounding my grandfather's death.

Reaching into my pocket now, I find that I've too many keys.

# *Fourteen*

Dickens had chosen the roof of a garage upon which to roost. It had a broken weather vane, rusted away to stillness. Once it'd been fashioned recognizably in the shape of a bird. There was some small comfort in that.

Wooden houses, three stories tall, rose on every side. Windows were alight in the kitchens, and Dickens could hear the sounds of people, their murmurings and laughter. He shuffled his feet on the wooden shingles of the garage roof, scrabbling up one side until he'd reached the spine where he crouched weary almost to death.

His purpose flickered in his breast, but the great fatigue he suffered threatened to swamp it altogether. He started sharply, his senses awakened by some warning. Listening with every nerve end as hard as he could seemed to drain the last pitiful shreds of his energy. There was nothing he could identify and he shuddered again to warm himself, settling to the rest he hoped would heal him.

The smell of overflowing garbage cans rose sickeningly to his nostrils, but he had no will to move away.

The cat was commonplace in appearance, a nondescript orange and white, the markings undistinguished. He showed evidence of a dozen battles fought and won. Scars across his muzzle gave him a look of permanent disdain, and one ear had nearly been chewed off in some old conflict. He was unprepossessing, but he was a survivor and knew the back alleys of his quarter of the town better than the humans who shared them with him.

He stalked along, picking his way as delicately as a lady afraid for the cleanliness of her skirts, head raised for the scent of some special treat that may have been thrown out at the end of someone's meal.

Suddenly he paused in mid-step. There was the odor of a warm living creature, a bird near by. Standing so, stock-still, a statue among the shadows, he fancied he could hear its pulse beat. He raised his head, the great yellow eyes blazing and deep. He saw the shape of Dickens crouching darkly against the sky on the spine of the garage roof.

The cat moved again, without haste but without any particular attempt to be stealthy. He knew his footfalls couldn't be heard above the low racket of the city. He reconnoitered the field and found his way to a fence that lay beside the low, squat building. He was on top of its slender width in one leap, all four feet well placed like a wire walker in the circus.

Dickens shook himself awake. There was danger close. He felt it nearing but couldn't move to fly away.

The cat stalked along the fence until it reached the lowest point of the eaves. He shifted his head from side to side, gathered himself close about his hind legs, and launched himself up high. He landed on the roof at Dickens's back, with not even the whisper of a sound.

The cat stepped daintily across the space. Dickens felt the presence behind him, hopped into the air and turned himself around before landing again. The cat struck in the moment, one foreleg reaching out for his prey, claws unsheathed. He stroked the air, trying to capture Dickens, who tumbled away. The clawed paw caught his eye and tore it from its place. Blood streamed down the side of Dickens's head. He saw a terrible scarlet blaze and screamed out in pain. He rolled, flapping and scratching, down the long slope of the roof and fell to the ground.

The cat raced along behind him and poised on the edge, peering down with his night-probing eyes. Dickens rolled away, finding a space beneath a plank of rotten wood. It was darker still inside the garage. The smell of gasoline clawed at his throat and tiny lungs. But he was safe for the moment.

He heard the cat clawing at the hole in the

wall. It screamed out in anger. Moments later it cried out again. A window slammed open. There was a shout and the cat fled away.

In Rochester my grandfather suffered another insult to his brain. It roused him from a troubled sleep, the pain of it giving him a voice that echoed down the empty hospital corridors.

The telephone rang at our house at nearly three o'clock in the morning. I didn't hear it, but I did hear the hushed but urgent sounds of my father getting dressed in the next room and whispering to my mother that she wasn't to get up. There was no need or no use for her to come to the hospital with him. I got up and went into their bedroom. He turned and saw me standing there and repeated to me in a normal voice that we weren't to come with him.

He smiled to reassure me, but it looked weak and tried to slip from his mouth. I think I started to cry then, because the next thing I knew my mother had me in her arms as she lay back on the pillows, treating me like the small boy I thought I no longer was.

The next day we went together to join my father at the hospital. He walked toward us down the harsh white hallway, his hair tousled, eyes heavy with lack of sleep, but smiling now in a stronger way.

"He's out of the woods. It was another stroke but he's out of the woods," he said.

I thought of the time I'd been lost in the woods and wanted to go to my grandfather right away so that I could tell him how brave I knew he'd been. But I did as I was told and went off to sit in a chair in the waiting room when Dr. Sand came in and took my father and mother aside to speak with them.

I learned then something of the way in which adult decisions are made. After much thought and discussion, deliberation and analysis, a final crisis comes and all the talk is seen to be no more than hopeful delay. The hope is swept away that all the prudent, serious consultation is proof that we are all responsible people secretly believing that fate won't strike the hammer blow if we at least appear busy taking care of our own problems. Within moments the disposition of the emergency is settled.

It was decided that Da wouldn't be kept in the hospital much longer. The nursing demands to come would be more than the institution was designed to handle. Nor was it practical for him to be taken home. There wasn't enough money to buy nursing care around the clock. And clearly too, he couldn't, at least for some long while, be taken to his son's house because both my mother and father needed their jobs more now than ever. He would have to go to a nursing home, a place of convalescence. I feared that for Da more than I'd ever feared anything in my life until that time.

We went in to see him at last. He lay

against the pillows much diminished in the early morning light. His eyes were on me, begging me to remember a promise.

It comes to me as I remember all of this that one of the clearest evidences of man's uniqueness is the exchange of promises, and the keeping of them.

Perhaps it is the fact that two human beings—or more—sometimes make a pact between them meant to confound and outwit the forces of expediency to do that which is right and proper against all odds.

Anyway such a covenant was made between Da and me.

# *Fifteen*

Knowing that the decision had been made, that Da, when he was somewhat recovered from this second attack, would be taken from the hospital, not to his own home or even to our house, but to a strange place where he would be "attended," disturbed me so that all thought of sleep, or even desire for it, left me.

I was quiet during the ride back home. I sat between my mother and father in the front seat of the car, felt overlooked and was glad of it.

My mother held a handkerchief to her mouth as though to trap any sobs that might break from it, but her eyes were dry as she stared out at the passing houses on the way home.

My father spoke in bits and pieces, mere comments on matters already accomplished, decisions made. As though the repetition of them would make them seem less terrible. There was a bitter sound of fear and helplessness in his voice as he insisted softly, more to himself than to anyone else, that a convalescent home was the best thing for Da. The only practical thing. The only sensible choice among many unhappy choices.

When we arrived home, my mother made a pot of coffee for them both and poured a glass of milk for me but, in the end, nobody touched their cups or glass. My father's eyes looked bruised in the yellow glow of the overhead light, my mother's deeply shadowed like someone's after a long mourning. They sent me off to bed.

I lay awake and shortly heard them making ready for their own bed, brushing their teeth and running the water in the bathroom sink. All the commonplace sounds of a household settling in for the night, somehow made hollow and echoing because of the knowledge that an old man wasn't at home, wasn't preparing for *his* own bed.

They retired. The springs stirred restlessly, and I knew they were as wakeful as I. Then, very thinly, I heard someone crying and, with a shock, realized that it was not my mother but my father. A moment later the door to their room was softly closed. Thinking back to that night I should imagine that my mother and father made love as proof against the sorrow that ravaged him.

I lay on my back staring at the patterns made by the moon upon the ceiling. There was nothing amusing or comforting I could imagine there as I'd done so often before. There were the calls of night creatures from outside the window. They seemed hushed and muted.

The clock in the living room below struck the hours. I heard them all, small vibrations through the hallway and stairwell. When it struck four, I got up with extra care. My bed made no sound when I took my weight from it, the chair made none as I sat on it to put on my socks and shoes. I dressed myself more quietly than I'd ever done before. There'd be no risk of awakening my father or mother behind their closed door.

I put on coat and cap and tiptoed down the hallway to the stairs. I went down along the side close to the wall so that the steps wouldn't creak. I let myself out into the first glow of false dawn that lit the eastern sky. It would go out before I reached my grandfather's house where my red wagon was kept.

Perhaps at that moment Dickens roused himself at sight of the pale finger of light that presented itself at the chink in the garage planking. He made his way back into the air, half dizzy, still exhausted but more determined than ever to fly to home.

He rose up in the air as the false dawn left the sky and plunged the world back into darkness. Crying softly against the pain, he gained the heights and waited, soaring there, for that bell-like whisper in his soul to guide him.

I walked along the silent streets of the town dragging the wagon behind me. One wheel made rhythmic little noises like the pipings of young birds. I went toward the hospital, fearing that someone would see me, a ten-year-old out on the dark early-morning streets, stop me, and take me home. A policeman, a milkman, some commuter up early for the journey to his job. But I met no one. It was as though only two people were awake in all the city. Myself and my grandfather waiting for me, sleepless, in a strange bed.

I approached the hospital by way of the park. I left the red wagon under the branches of a maple tree and walked across the silent street. I stood on the sidewalk outside my grandfather's room. The curtains were closed but I knew that he was inside, lying facing the window, trying to see through them. I looked both ways along the walk. There was nobody around. I stepped across the flowerbed between the sidewalk and the building and tried to test the window to see if it could be raised. It was locked tight. I tapped on the window with my fingernails in the way that a chick taps upon the inside of its egg, alerting Da to my coming.

Down along the way, about twenty feet, was a side entrance to the hospital. I knew it entered on to the waiting room and the corridor that led to my grandfather's room.

It was locked as well. I went across the street and returned with the wagon, its slender squeaking arousing the birds for a moment before they settled themselves again. Their chattering lifted my spirits. I left the wagon among some bushes growing beside the door.

There was no one about the front of the building. Bright lights flooded the reception area and I could see a woman in a white uniform sitting behind the counter. She looked bored and tired, the way people do who are awake when everyone else is asleep. She was making some sort of entries in a book, glancing up at the clock on the wall above the door to her left. She shifted restlessly, put down her pen and got up to stretch. She seemed to be making up her mind about something, then picked up her purse and disappeared through a door at the back.

I slipped through the front door and ran across the linoleum to the corridor. My rubber-soled Keds made little squeaking noises that I hoped couldn't be heard very far. I looked into the hallway through the little square of glass set in the door and, seeing that it was empty, opened it noiselessly and was inside. The antiseptic smell of the place scared me. I walked down the hall, being careful now to make no sound at all. A door swung open on one side of the corridor up ahead of me, and I ducked into a little alcove that housed a drinking fountain. There was space enough to hide me.

I saw a nurse, her attention on a chart in her hands, walk down a side turning. I crept along until I was opposite the joining and saw her sitting at a desk, reading the chart in the glow of a desk lamp that did little to brighten the gloom. I was across the juncture in a wink. I passed the foyer to the side door to my right, the waiting room to my left. I was at Da's door.

Just as I'd expected, his back was turned to me as he lay in bed, his head toward the window. I went around that side between the bed and window. He was lying there, his eyes wide, looking very pale but charged with determination. He moved his right hand out from beneath the covers and reached out to me. I took his hand and he smiled—or tried to.

I took the blanket and sheet from him, uncovering his big-boned body now seeming much diminished even to a child's eyes. He'd lost considerable weight. He made scrabbling attempts to move, wanting to straighten, to roll over upon the bed in such a way that his feet would fall to the floor and he'd be sitting up on his own. But he failed. I put his arm about my shoulder, kneeling beside the bed, squirmed until my body was under his, my head against his chest, and straightened up. He tottered and nearly fell the other way but threw out his right arm, stiffly, with sudden strength, and we posed there for a moment. We'd come that far, but I was already lost for any way to go further. I'd have to bring the wagon inside.

"Can you sit here for a minute, Da?" I asked.

He nodded, and I saw a muscle arch along his jaw, a trick of his when he prepared himself for any effort, large or small.

I placed his other arm at his side, his hand on the bed, and left him there supported by the tripod of his arms and spine, motionless.

I hurried out into the hallway, after first peeking out to make certain the nurse wasn't roaming about, and went through the small foyer to the side door. It opened easily from within and I propped it open with the kickstop at the bottom. I got the wagon from the bush and started into the hospital. The shrill whine of the wheel, which sounded like no more than a bird's call in the out-of-doors, was sharp and loud within the echoing walls of the hospital.

I lifted the wagon in my arms, settled it so that the handle wouldn't swing around and make a crash, and crept back with it to my grandfather's room.

He was still seated on the edge of the bed, steady as a rock. I set the wagon down on the floor near his feet.

It was a struggle to get his arms in the sleeves of his bathrobe, but it was done at last. I tied it around his waist with the tassled cord, then I bent and put on his socks and slippers. I straightened up and looked at him, smiling to let him know that things were moving along famously. His eyes twinkled and he made a movement with his mouth. I looked to the bedside table for a glass and his teeth, but they weren't there. His hand moved on the sheet, a finger pointing to the cabinet within the table. I found his teeth there and placed them in his mouth. He managed a broad grin and I had to laugh softly for the curious adventure we were off upon.

Now came the part of greatest difficulty. I

helped him slide forward on the high bed until his feet were on the floor. I draped his arms over my shoulders one after the other. Looking up into his face, I saw a sudden spurt of fear in his eyes, not of pain or injury but that we might fail. I took a deep breath, my hands behind his back, and urged his weight to fall forward on me. We danced in each other's embrace for a terrible moment, his slippers shuffling on the tile, and then I turned him around and had him poised above the wagon bed.

"Bend your knees, Da," I whispered. He did so. He became heavier as his weight fell away from me. I staggered and nearly lost my hold. He fell, more than sat, into the wagon.

I was drenched with sweat. I would have laughed at Da if we'd been playing because he looked foolish sitting in a child's wagon. But we weren't playing and he looked, instead, quite brave and proud of what we'd accomplished so far.

I went behind him and tried to pull him back farther on the bed of the wagon, but it rolled back on my toes. I threw a pillow under the wheels to block them and, taking him under the arms, managed it a second time. Then I lifted his legs so that he was completely settled in it, his knees raised almost to his chin. I placed each hand on a side of the wagon. He held on, his jaw flexing with the effort.

I pulled the wagon with great effort to the door, peeked out, saw no one, and somehow managed to get my grandfather in the wagon out of his room. I hauled it to the open door and out into the night air. His weight had stilled the squeaky wheel. I shivered when the chill struck me. In a moment the door was closed and locked again behind us.

Placing my hands behind my back, I lifted the handle of the wagon and, facing forward, pulled for home toward Da's house a good mile away. I trudged along the dark streets. The sky began to lighten. The trees and bushes were no longer dark, featureless shapes; there was a tinge of color here and there against the gray of the dawning. An automobile, headlamps glowing, passed along the streets from time to time, but no one stopped to ask what a boy was doing pulling an old man, dressed in robe and slippers, in a child's wagon, along the empty streets.

It seemed to take forever; the sun was rising above the low hills to the east, long morning shadows slanting across the road in front of me, the grass of lawns still wet with dew. Some householders came out on their porches to get the milk or morning paper. I knew a few of them and raised my head to say hello, good morning, or something to deflect their questions, but no one asked me anything or tried to stop me in any way. Perhaps they sensed, somehow, what I was doing.

I trudged along, dragging Da in the wagon behind me, the wheel singing a monotonous little song, smelling the new morning, hearing the birds waking to the day. We reached the

saltbox by the rushing stream that fed the
Genesee. I dragged the wagon around the back
and dropped the handle. I'd never been so
weary in my life.

Da was looking at me, a kind of pity for
my pain mixed with pride for my courage in his
eyes. I found the key to the back door in the
flowerpot upon the outside windowsill and
opened the door. I pulled the wagon into the
mud room, into the kitchen, through the living
room to the foot of the stairs. Tears piled up
behind my eyes. How would I ever lift him up
the many steps?

Da spoke. I understood the terrible gibberish. It was the familiar bed, not so much the
room, he sought. I went upstairs and took the
mattress from the bed, dragged it down the
stairs and out back to the screened summer
porch. I returned for sheets and blankets, pillows and cases. When the bed was made up as
well as I knew how, I pulled the wagon up beside it.

Da sort of let go then. I realized, all at
once, the terrible effort it must have taken to
have him sit up in the jouncing little wagon
all that way. He tumbled out of the wagon onto
the bed. I pushed and pulled him as gently as I
could. He helped with crablike motions of legs
and arms until I had him settled on the mattress on the floor of the summer porch. I placed
his head on the pillows and brushed the thin
hair from his eyes. He made uncomfortable
sounds with his mouth. I went to get a glass of

water, gave him a little to drink, then took his teeth and placed them in what was left. He smiled with his lips closed tight. He held out his hand in gratitude. I took it and he squeezed mine. Not very hard. He had so little strength left.

The tears dammed up in me wouldn't wait anymore. Before I turned away, I saw his own eyes close in deep content. I ran out to the pigeon lofts. The tears poured out of me. I wailed like a baby, leaning up against the house filled with beautiful birds. After a time I dried my eyes and was about to start the chores, to let the pigeons fly.

I looked off to the house that was my grandfather's. He was safe in it for as long as he yet should live. The sun topped the chimney and sent a blaze of glory into my eyes. I turned them away and sought the western sky.

There was a moving dot far away. As I watched, it grew larger, moving erratically across the blue. I felt my heart squeeze small and then expand till it filled my chest.

"Oh, Da," I heard myself cry. "Look! Look! Look there in the reaches of the sky!"

The dot grew larger and larger. It was white and grizzle blue. Larger and larger. I cried out again and again.

"Dickens! Dickens!"

Dickens had come home, his race lost but flown faithfully to its end.

# *Epilogue*

That's really quite all of the story of that race and those fateful days when I was a boy of ten.

My grandfather died in his bed at home—upstairs in the bedroom where his children had been born and his wife had passed away—not long after that morning when Dickens came home.

Dickens lived only a few months longer, then surrendered to the terrible trials, depletions, and wounds suffered on that gallant flight. He died at home.

It's dark now, the day is done. There is a different quality to the dark that comes after the setting of the sun and that which precedes the rising of it. Perhaps there are sounds and smells left over from the day that alter it. Perhaps a different texture to the winds.

Whatever the case, one is sensed as a beginning and the other as an ending.